In Honor

Also by Jessi Kirby

Moonglass

Golden

In Honor

Jessi Kirby

SIMON & SCHUSTER BFYR

New York London Toronto Sydney New Delhi

An imprint of Simon & Schuster Children's Publishing Division
1230 Avenue of the Americas, New York, New York 10020

This book is a work of fiction. Any references to historical events, real people, or real places are used fictitiously. Other names, characters, places, and events are products of the author's imagination, and any resemblance to actual events or places or persons, living or dead, is entirely coincidental.

For information about special discounts for bulk purchases, please contact Simon & Schuster Special Sales at 1-866-506-1949 or business@simonandschuster.com.

The Simon & Schuster Speakers Bureau can bring authors to your live event. For more information or to book an event, contact the Simon & Schuster Speakers Bureau at 1-866-248-3049 or visit our website at www.simonspeakers.com.

Also available in a SIMON & SCHUSTER BFYR hardcover edition
Book design by Krista Vossen
The text for this book is set in Bembo.
Manufactured in the United States of America
First SIMON & SCHUSTER BFYR paperback edition May 2013
2 4 6 8 10 9 7 5 3 1
The Library of Congress has cataloged the hardcover edition as follows:
Kirby, Jessi.
In honor / Jessi Kirby. — 1st ed.
p. cm.
Summary: Three days after she learns that her brother, Finn, died serving in Iraq, Honor receives a letter from him asking her to drive his car from Texas to California for a concert, and when his estranged best friend shows up suddenly and offers to accompany her, they set off on a road trip that reveals much about all three of them.
ISBN 978-1-4424-1697-0 (hardcover)
[1. Grief—Fiction. 2. Automobile travel—Fiction. 3. Brothers and sisters—Fiction. 4. Orphans—Fiction.] I. Title.
PZ7.K633522In 2012
[Fic]—dc23
2011030542
ISBN 978-1-4424-1698-7 (pbk)
ISBN 978-1-4424-1699-4 (eBook)

For Schuyler.
This book is truly as much yours
as it is mine.

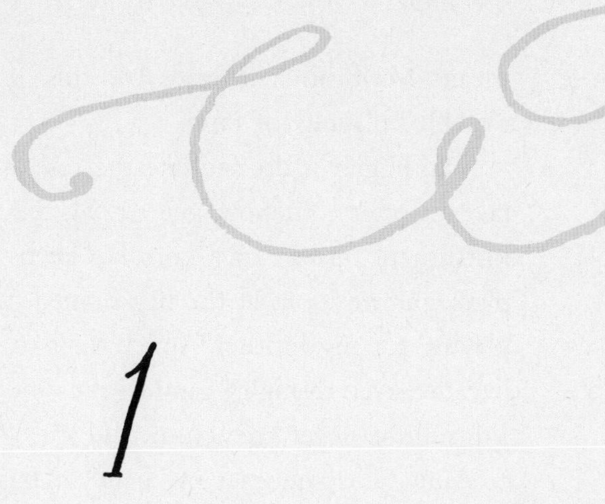

1

The snap of the first shot breaks open the afternoon. I squeeze my eyes shut and wait for the second one, ears strained against the silence. Seven rifles have come together as one, in salute of Finn. With the second crack, I open my eyes and focus on the youngest of the riflemen, who stands on the end. His gloved hands had trembled as he'd lifted his rifle, but now they are steady, firm. A third shot. Rifles are brought back to the shoulders of their bearers, and the general bends, fingers brushing the grass, and picks up three of the gleaming spent shells. I stand there, stiff as the troopers, while my aunt cries softly beside me.

The bugler steps forward and licks his lips before he lifts his trumpet. It occurs to me that I've never actually heard taps played in real life. As the first notes emerge, I try to be present in the moment, try to press into my mind what this moment means. My brother is dead. And this . . . this song means it's real. He's playing for Finn.

The bugler is dressed like the rest of the soldiers, but his face is softer somehow, gentler. Maybe because he holds an instrument instead of a gun. He keeps his eyes open as he plays, and he looks at the flag-draped casket the entire time, playing for my brother. And I want to tell him about Finn because, even though I can feel the emotion behind his song, I'm sure he never knew him.

Aunt Gina squeezes my hand so hard it hurts while she tries to muffle her sobs. I press my lips together, gulp back my own. One of us should. Finn would be proud of that. He always told me to look strong, even if I didn't feel it, because sometimes that's all you can do.

The troopers let the last notes of the song drift off and settle into the distance before they step forward for the flag. They lift it gingerly off the casket and fold it once, twice, before the general tucks the shells within the waves of red and white. Then eleven more folds, until all that's left is a rigid triangle of white stars on blue. The young trooper, probably my brother's age, hands it to the general for inspection.

The general is a somber man in his forties, dark hair peppered with gray. He takes the flag and steps forward, looking from my aunt to me. But his gaze settles on me when he walks across the damp grass, and now my knees weaken. I don't know if Gina has arranged this or if it's because I'm listed as Finn's only next of kin, but the general stops in front of me. His eyes speak of sorrow, and as he stands there, I wonder how many times he's had to do this in his career.

He recites words I hear but don't really listen to: "On

behalf of the President of the United States, the Commandment of the Marine Corps, and a grateful nation, please accept this flag as a symbol of our appreciation for your loved one's service to Country and Corps."

As he talks, I am grateful that my parents never had to stand here and bury their son, but I mourn the fact a million times over that I'm here to do it alone. As soon as the flag leaves the general's hands and is in my own, I clutch it to my chest like it's Finn himself, and now I can't look strong. I didn't think I had it in me to cry more than I have in the last two weeks, but the tears flow immediately, and when they do, the general seems to step out from behind his uniform to grieve with me. We stand there, me locked within the circle of his brass and patches, and he means it as a comfort, but it's all rigid corners and stiff fabric.

I whisper "thank you," then pull back, and he squeezes my shoulders before letting go. Aunt Gina steps forward and puts her arms around me, and the general and his troopers fall away. Faces of people—my friends and Finn's, his teachers, coaches, classmates, our whole town—stream by, puffy-eyed and heartbroken, offering their condolences. When it's Lilah's turn, she doesn't say anything, but she hugs me hard and that says everything. More people come by us to pay their respects, and we stand there for what feels like an eternity, nodding, thanking them for coming, until they've all gone.

Aunt Gina excuses herself to talk with the funeral director, and I have a moment to myself. I don't want to look at the casket waiting to be lowered into the ground next to our parents, so I walk over to our bench, the one Finn and I would sit on when we came to visit, and I sit down, still hugging the flag to my chest. And that's when I see a silhouette I recognize, standing off some distance—one I didn't realize was missing from the stream of faces until now.

Rusty stands there looking like a grown man. He's in a proper suit and tie, his hair combed back, and he would look perfectly respectable if not for the paper-wrapped bottle dangling from his hand. I wonder who told him. I hadn't even thought of calling him, but then, I wouldn't have known how to get ahold of him anyway. He and Finn hadn't spoken since Finn enlisted, and it wasn't like we were friends anymore.

Still.

He'd come, and that meant something. Even if he watched from a distance. I want to walk over and tell him that him being there would've meant more to Finn than anyone else. That whatever differences they'd had were long forgotten. But when I get up, he raises the bottle to his lips for a long pull, then turns and walks away. Just like he did over a year ago.

2

I was alone.

After the last car had pulled out of the parking lot and Aunt Gina had wrapped a weary arm around my shoulders, I'd told her I wanted to stay at the cemetery awhile longer. She didn't argue. Didn't say *anything*. Just pulled me in for a hug that was so drenched in sadness, I thought I might drown right there on the still-warm asphalt, even though there was no water around for miles. I'd untangled myself as delicately as I could and told her I just needed to say my good-byes, which was nowhere near true.

How could I? Doing that would mean I'd have to give up my thin thread of hope that there was still a chance I could wake up the next morning and find Finn sitting on the couch watching *SportsCenter*, pouring bowl after bowl of Golden Grahams into the same sweet, lukewarm milk. It would mean

I'd have to face the stillness of his bedroom, knowing that the clothes hanging in the closet would never be worn again, the football on his dresser never tossed absently between his hands while he pretended to listen to me talk.

So I didn't say any good-byes. I just sat there on our bench, like we'd done together so many times before, until the first stars twinkled in the dusky purple sky. But there by myself, in the unfolding coolness of the evening, those times with Finn seemed impossibly far away. I stayed anyway, watching star after star blink distant and impassive like nothing had changed, and I tried to tell myself the same thing Finn had told me on the nights I missed our parents the most. He'd bring me to this bench, where we could see their headstones, and tell me that looking up at the stars was a way to look right back into the past—back to when our mom tucked us in each night and our dad chased away bad dreams and we all ate biscuits and gravy for breakfast every Sunday.

He'd say it was true because by the time the light from those stars twinkled all the way down to us, it was years and years old. He figured that when we sat side by side watching the night sky stretch endless and sparkling above us, our parents were there with us too, because it was the same light that had shone down on them their whole lives. Back then, I'd believed it with everything in me.

But not tonight. Tonight I was sitting there alone, watching the stars blur in and out of focus, trying to feel something besides the crushing loneliness of the cemetery. He couldn't be gone. I needed him too much. I needed him for all the little ways he'd make me feel better whenever I was sad or upset or lost.

He hated when I cried, and so he'd do his best to distract me however he could. When we were little, that meant riding me on his handlebars down to the Stop-N-Go for candy. As we got older, it meant taking me out to the garage with a Coke, so he could work on his car while I leaned against it, handing him tools and telling him how so and so gave me a dirty look or how sure I was that no boy was ever gonna like me. If it was really bad, he'd let me tag along with him and Rusty for burgers or give me and Lilah the car for the night so we could go see a movie. They were all small things, really. But I knew I'd always have him to tell me what to say or how to do something or which direction to go in. He was my constant and my guide. Without him, I was beyond lost.

By the time I got home, Aunt Gina was asleep on the couch, still in her funeral clothes, and the house was silent. In the kitchen, I opened the fridge, though I had no intention of eating. Inside, it was bursting with the foil-covered casseroles and lasagnas people had brought over because that's what you do when someone dies. Which was a nice gesture, but I hadn't felt much like eating since the notification officer and chaplain had knocked on our door to inform us that Finn had been killed in action, that they were deeply sorry, and that arrangements were being made to fly his remains home.

His remains. You'd think they'd be trained to say something different.

I shut the fridge and stood in the middle of the kitchen, listening to the clock tick away the seconds. The answering machine blinked one new message, and I knew it would be Lilah, calling to see if she could come over one last time before she left for school. She'd put off leaving for her college orientation as soon as I got news about Finn, and she'd taken up her post as my best friend and caretaker since then.

If I wanted company, she came over and we watched stupid movies or flipped through endless issues of *Us Weekly* and *People* until I could fall asleep. If she could tell I needed a little time, she dropped by with dinner her mom had made, enough for Aunt Gina and me, then came back the next day, ready for whatever mood I was in. A few times she just sat on my bed and cried with me, but really I knew she was crying *for* me. She had a certain kind of empathy not many people possess. She'd done the same when we were four years old and I had just lost my parents. She felt my pains like they were her own, and I did the same for her.

I had no way to tell her how much all of this meant and how much I was gonna miss her when we headed in opposite directions on the map. And I couldn't tell her how leaving for Austin and my dream college suddenly felt as meaningless as the days that stretched out in front of me, empty and full at the same time with Finn's death. He'd been the one to show me UTA in the first place when I tagged along on one of his football recruiting trips. I had no idea I'd fall head over heels for it, but I did. I didn't even bother to apply anywhere else, because I was so sure that school was where I belonged. Only now, I wasn't sure of anything. How was I supposed to go off to college and start a new life when my brother's had just ended so abruptly? It seemed wrong.

But I couldn't tell Lilah any of this, because you're supposed to be happy when you go off to college—excited, elated, all of those words that mean you're about to do something big and amazing. And I wanted her to be, at least. It was finally time for us to get out of town and go start our lives for real, and she deserved to be happy about it. I couldn't talk to her tonight, before she left. I wouldn't be able to hold it together. She knew me well enough to know how much I cared about her, and I knew her well enough to know she'd understand. I promised myself that when I was ready and she was gone and settled into school, I'd sit down and write her a good, long letter and tell her everything.

A letter.

I glanced over at the little round table in the corner of the kitchen, and it was still there, untouched, which was no miracle since it was only me and Aunt Gina.

Three days after the knock on our door, I'd come in from a walk with Lilah, actually laughing over a story about Finn, and then in an instant, all the air whooshed right out of me. Sitting on the kitchen table was an envelope, addressed to me, in his handwriting. I stared at it. Lilah put her hand on my shoulder, tentative.

"Oh, Honor . . . ," she started. "He must've sent it before . . . and probably no one knew. . . ."

I'd stepped toward it like it was a sleeping animal I didn't want to disturb. Picked up the envelope. Run my thumb over the address, over Finn's writing. And then put it down in the exact same spot and backed away. "I can't. . . ." Looked at Lilah. "You wanna go out for a while? We can drive the Pala this time." She'd nodded quickly, and we walked straight back out the door. I didn't go in the kitchen much after that.

The thing was, Finn didn't write letters. He wrote e-mails,

once a week. And every time I got one from him, I'd give him a hard time about writing me a *real* letter, with *real* thoughts, instead of just telling me it was all "fine" over there and how the dusty desert wasn't all that different from central Texas, and how combat drills reminded him of football. I wanted him to tell me the truth, even if it was a hard truth, because those things are too heavy to carry alone. He'd always been that person to me, the one I could tell everything to, and I liked to think I could be the same for him. But once he made up his mind to enlist instead of go to college and play football, it felt like he decided I couldn't.

Lilah said he was trying to protect me and that I should just let it go, but it sat like a rock in my gut and I tried to tell him as much. I wanted him to know he didn't have to be so sunny and upbeat all the time—that it was okay to be honest, for once, about how it really was, and if he was scared or wished he'd never gone.

Which was why I hadn't opened the letter.

I was afraid, when I saw it, of what I'd find. And now, especially after the fact, I didn't want to know that he'd been scared or lonely or homesick, because any one of those things would be enough to break what was left of me. Now I *needed* to keep thinking he'd been happy over there and it wasn't as bad as I imagined.

But he'd written it, a real letter. I owed it to him to read it.

I glanced through the doorway into the living room at Gina, who seemed to have aged twenty years in the last two weeks. Her blond hair fell loose and dull around her face, and her chest moved rhythmically up and down beneath her wrinkled black blouse. She didn't flinch at the sound when I slid a chair out and sat at the table. I picked the envelope up, surprised at the thickness of it between my fingers. A deep breath didn't feel near enough to prepare me for reading whatever he'd written, but I drew one in anyway then slid my finger under the top flap and tore up through the seam of the envelope. I exhaled once more before I brought out the folded pages and opened them to read.

Dear H—

First off, I know this is gonna get to you late—that's just the way things work around here, but I'm hoping that since I'm finally sending you a "real letter" you won't hold it against me.

I wish more than anything I could've come home to see you graduate, tried every which way to figure it out, but there was just no way that was gonna happen. But you have to know how damn proud of you I am. Mom and Dad would've been too, you know. So proud.

And now you got a wide-open road ahead of you with nothing standing in your way. I hope by now you're all packed up and ready for school. It's a big thing, you know. You better go and do it up right or I'll have to come back there just to kick your ass into gear. There's a big world out there and I'm seeing it now—the good and the bad. And you will too. Have a few adventures while you're out there. Put your feet in the ocean. Watch the stars disappear into morning. Then when I get back we'll compare notes.

How's that for a "real letter"? Everything you thought it'd be? Wise and inspiring, since it's on paper? I tried. Just so you know, that took me twice as long as an e-mail would have. Hope you're happy.

Love,
Finn

PS — Do me a favor—next time you see Kyra Kelley, make sure you tell her all about your handsome older brother.

Something deep in my chest unhinged. Overflowed. Tore through every little space in me until I thought I might burst. It was so Finn, so what he'd say, that I let myself think for a second that he wasn't actually gone. I ran my finger over the indentations of his pen strokes. He had no idea when he wrote it that I would sit at our kitchen table and read it after his funeral, or that I wouldn't laugh or shake my head but weep as quietly as I could, so I wouldn't wake Gina.

Hot tears cut silent paths down my cheeks. I set the letter down on the table and wiped the wetness from my face. The seconds ticked away in the heat of the evening, and the pages in front of me fluttered lightly beneath the lazy current of the ceiling fan.

Pages. There were more than one. After another deep breath, I gently lifted the one with his handwriting on it away from the two behind it, almost afraid of what they might be. And seated alone at the kitchen table, in the sad quiet of the house, I laughed when I saw.

I laughed out loud, but without any sort of joy, because this had to be a joke. All of it. The car accident that took my parents, the hand-rigged bomb that took my brother, and now this. A letter he had to have sent to me months ago, when the road really was wide open, and the two tickets to Kyra Kelley's farewell concert were the perfect punch line to his PS joke.

He would've written that last line with a smile, knowing I'd get it as soon as I looked at the printouts. He would've known I'd stare at the seat numbers wondering how, from half a world away, he'd managed to get tickets to her very last show. And he probably would have pictured Lilah and me going nuts over them, then immediately shifting into planning mode for the trip out to California for the concert.

But really, it should've been me and him.

When I turned fourteen, he surprised me with a trip in the Impala all the way down to Austin to see her sing, and I swore she smiled at us in the front row. When I turned sixteen, he let me drive to the show in San Antonio, and when she looked our way more than once, I decided she remembered us. Miles of road and gallon after gallon of gas were the links between me and Finn and Kyra Kelley.

If he was the guide in my life, she was the soundtrack. In my mind, we'd all three grown up together. I loved her from her very first album, and Finn did too, though eventually he stopped admitting it. She was sweet and earnest and wrote her own songs. Songs about getting her heart broken by boys who didn't know she existed or who were in love with girls all wrong for them. She wrote my life, and I loved her for it.

I followed in magazines her transformation from country girl to pop crossover, to graceful twenty-something singer-turned-model-turned-actress. I watched her get her heart broken some more and thought she deserved better. Someone good and solid like my brother, who would open doors for her and look out for her heart. The kind of guy who would surprise his little sister with an impossibly perfect gift and ask only one thing in return.

Tell her about him.

The thought grabbed at me, and I glanced over at Aunt Gina, who was still sleeping. Even when the chaplain had informed us that Finn's services would need to be held the day before I was supposed to leave for school, she'd insisted—forcefully—that I not change my plans. And there was something in her voice that warned me not to argue. Life had to go on, she'd said. She needed to get back to work to pay the bills. I needed to go to school like we'd all talked about. The best way to honor Finn was to do that. We had to do these things, because otherwise this huge, gaping loss would swallow us, and life would keep right on going whether we did or not.

I'd been furious at her for saying those things that sounded so callous, but she knew better than anyone how true they were. She'd buried my mom and dad—her sister and brother-in-law, then took us in and kept going the best she could. And now she expected me to do the same. But on the pages in front of me, Finn had given me a gift. And a final request. I had five days to honor it.

I eyed Gina once more and made a silent promise that

after I did this one thing, this one thing that Finn had asked, I would keep going, right to school. Getting to Kyra Kelley would mean missing orientation week, but I quickly justified it. I'd make it back in time for the start of classes, and Gina would be none the wiser. I hated the idea of lying to her, but there was no way I could tell her what I really meant to do before life could go on. I couldn't say that I was going to take the tickets he'd given me, get in the Impala, and drive it out to California so I could see Kyra Kelley. She'd think I lost my mind.

Nervous resolve settled over me. I folded the letter and tickets and tucked them back in the envelope, slid it into my purse, and woke Gina to tell her a plan I hoped she'd believe: that I was going to do just what she said; that when she woke up the next morning and left for work, determined to keep going, I would get in Finn's car, point it straight toward Austin, and I would keep going too.

3

It was early, but the vinyl seats were already hot against the backs of my legs when I slid in. I'd be driving with the windows down for sure, probably barefoot before noon. My fingers found the lever under the seat, and I popped the trunk to load the stuff I'd piled next to the car—the contents of my life packed into a few boxes and a duffel bag. I'd packed most of it weeks ago in giddy anticipation of the day I'd drive off to my new life in Austin. At the moment, though, that was a distant thought on the edge of my mind. I slammed the trunk shut and breathed in the morning air, which was already heavy with August heat. This was stupid. Ridiculous for sure. But Finn hadn't ever asked me for anything. And now this was something. He'd want me to go. He'd think it was a great big adventure, a crazy story I could tell later on.

Sun glinted off the corner of the hood, looking like a

white spot on its shiny black surface, and I thought of oil. I needed to check the oil. And the water, so I didn't fry the engine in the middle of the desert. I propped the hood open and pulled out the dipstick, which looked all right. Under the radiator cap, the water hovered around the fill line. Everything else seemed fine, but Finn had always turned the car on to listen for anything *off*. I had no idea what I'd be listening for, but it couldn't hurt. When I leaned in and turned the key, the rumble rippled through the quiet.

"Sounds like shit, you know." I knew the voice instantly.

He'd come out of nowhere. I ducked my head out the door and stood up slowly, trying to decide how to answer. Rusty stood in the same suit I'd seen him in at the service, but now his shirt hung untucked and his tie was gone. He still had the bottle in his hand, though, and from the looks of it, he was still drunk. Not funny-drunk Rusty, as I'd seen him so many times, but surly drunk. Probably freshly failed-out-of-school drunk.

"You reek," I said, pushing past him to look at the engine.

He turned his head in slow motion to follow me, then took another pull from his bottle and swallowed hard. "Maybe. But the real issue, *Honor*, is that you were supposed to be taking care of her for Finn." He surveyed the car, hood to trunk. "I don't think he'd be too happy with this." He swayed, then focused his eyes right at me, and in that second I couldn't stand him. I'd heard he'd gone and partied his football chances away, but I didn't imagine it'd be this bad.

"Yeah? Well, he'd be disgusted with you right now." I took a step closer, then immediately regretted it when his thick, boozy breath hit me. "You're a wreck, Rusty. Following right in your dad's footsteps, I see." I nodded at the bottle, but he didn't say anything, so I kept going. "The least you could have done was show up at your best friend's funeral sober. *He* would have." Guilt stung inside me somewhere. I'd known Rusty for so long, I knew exactly where to hit him: Compare him to his dad, and compare him with my brother. One he hated, the other he'd looked up to as much as I had.

He set his bottle on top of the car, stared past me with bloodshot eyes, then stumbled to the open hood and leaned in. I didn't move. This all felt so, so wrong. Finn would have hated this. He would have hated Rusty this way and me so angry. He would've found a way to smooth it over like he'd always done with everything.

Rusty yanked at something, and the rumble of the engine jumped noticeably louder. He stood back and nodded to himself, then seemed to remember I was standing there. "Carburetor needed more air. No point driving around in a muscle car when it doesn't sound like one."

I looked at the ground, silent, and kicked a piece of gravel with the toe of my boot. "Right." I leaned back on the side of the car, and he shut the hood and ambled over next to me after grabbing up his bottle again.

"You goin' somewhere?" He nodded to the cab, where a creased map sat on the bench seat, and now I was sure he'd flunked out. He didn't even realize it was time for school to be starting up. Good. No need for me to mention it.

I blew a wisp of hair off my forehead. "Just getting out of town for a little while."

He nodded, then stifled a burp. "You got family elsewhere?"

"No."

"Boyfriend?" I shook my head but didn't look at him. He took another drink, then leaned in too close. "Where you going then, H?"

"Nowhere." I pushed off the car and walked around to the passenger side, opened the door, and rearranged my stuff. There was no way I was actually gonna say it out loud to Rusty. It'd be an open invitation for him to make fun of me. Even in my own mind, it still sounded ridiculous. Going to Kyra Kelley's last concert to tell her about my dead brother? Because he sent me tickets? Not the thing I wanted to share with anyone, especially Rusty. But it was something to hold close to me, a goal for the moment in the middle of the hazy emptiness all around. A plan.

When our parents died, Finn was five years old. Even then, he'd figured out a way to deal with it. Gina said that from that moment on, he never stopped moving or playing or planning. He was always busy with something, and he kept me busy too, like if we both always had something to do, we wouldn't ever have to be sad. And he continued with it, always. He focused on concrete things he could accomplish. In high school it was grades and football and his car. It was why the Impala was in mint condition. He'd worked on it every day since he got it, telling me about all the places it'd take us one day. And I'd sat inside, breathing in the smell of old vinyl and thinking how I'd never want to go anywhere without him. Now here I was again, in the cab of the car, thinking the same thing, but about to do it anyway.

Rusty ducked his head into the cab on the driver's side and turned the engine off. Then he slid in behind the wheel and looked at me with quickly sobering eyes. "Where you goin'?"

I tucked my map beneath the seat and rolled up the *Us Weekly*. "It wouldn't make sense to you."

He raised an eyebrow. "Not much that does these days. Try me."

I sat down, eyes on the dash. Maybe he'd leave if I told him. Or maybe he'd somehow understand and think it was a great idea. I looked right at him, drunk and disheveled, and mustered what confidence I could. "I'm going to California to see Kyra Kelley's last concert." It sounded infinitely more ridiculous than I'd anticipated. I waited. He looked me over, bemused, and for a second I thought maybe he was too wasted to realize the idiocy of what I'd just said. I fumbled, trying to make it make sense to him. "To tell her about Finn. He sent me these tickets. And then he asked me to tell her about him."

He nodded reverently, and for a second I thought in some tiny way he got it. Then he leaned over, put his hands on my cheeks, and smooshed them together. "That . . . is the dumbest thing I've ever heard." I smacked at his hands, and he let go and leaned back against the seat, laughing.

I hated him. I hated him for the way he showed up yesterday, for showing up here today, for being a mess and making fun of me, and for not being Finn when I needed him most. My brother was everything he wasn't. There'd been plenty of times I'd wondered how they were friends, because they were so different, and now I didn't care.

"Get out, Rusty." I shoved him, and he almost toppled out the door, which made him laugh even harder. I crossed my arms over my chest, willing myself not to cry in front of him.

He sucked in a deep breath and tried to get ahold of himself, I could tell, but I refused to look over at him. Finally, he put a hand on my knee. "I'm sorry, H, I'm sorry. That just sounds like—"

"I know what it sounds like. All right? I know. But I don't know what else to do right now, and Lilah just left for school, and Gina's telling me I have to move on, and he wrote me this letter and sent me these tickets. And the last thing he said to me was to tell Kyra Kelley about him. That was the last thing he asked me to do." Tears came now, but I didn't care. I was already humiliated. "So I'm gonna go to her concert and do that. And yes, I realize how stupid it sounds, okay? But you don't get to have an opinion about it."

I got out and heaved the passenger door shut, then wiped my eyes and walked around to the driver's side, where he sat, finger tapping the steering wheel, stunned-quiet. "So get out. I need to get on the road." He didn't move. "Rusty, come on."

He waved me off. "All right, all right." But he didn't get out. Instead, he shoved my stuff onto the floorboard and scooted over to the passenger side. "I'm going too, then."

"Like hell you are."

He stretched out his legs in front of him. "Yep. Finn wouldn'ta wanted you going off by yourself like this." He patted the dash. "What if the car breaks down? Or you get lost?" I didn't move, and I didn't say anything. He leaned his head back. "What're you waitin' for, H? Let's go see what's-her-name. I'll just take a little rest here while you drive." He patted the seat, then grinned up at me with half-closed eyes before his chin fell to his chest and he was out.

I wasn't getting him out of the car. I thought for a second about driving to his house and rolling him out onto his front yard, but I didn't hate him enough to leave him like that to deal with his dad. And what if the car *did* break down or I *did* get lost? What then? I glanced down at him in the passenger seat, where he'd ridden alongside my brother for all of high school. Then I turned around and went in the house, to Finn's room.

Inside, it was still and dark. I twisted open the blinds and stood by the window a moment, feeling almost like I was doing something wrong. Like it should all be left exactly as it was even though I'd been in there a handful of times in the nine months since he'd shipped out. He'd always kept it simple and neat. It didn't make much of a statement about him. He saved the Impala for that. From the chrome on the wheels to the slick black paint that cost him a fortune, he poured himself into that car. *That* was where I'd gone to feel close to him when he left. Driving around in it had been a comfort, so maybe it was right that I was about to take it on a mission that made sense only to me.

What didn't make sense was that I'd made up my mind, somewhere between the car and Finn's room, that Rusty could go with me. And that he'd need some clothes, because he reeked of a night spent drinking and mourning. I'd been so angry with him outside, I hadn't let myself think of how he must be feeling. Finn would have been destroyed if it'd been the other way around.

I went to his dresser and pulled out a few shirts and a pair of jeans. Outside of his uniform or practice clothes, Rusty'd always worn boots and long pants, even in the Texas summer heat. But since we were headed to California, I went ahead and grabbed a pair of Finn's shorts and a pair of flip-flops for him, just in case. He could figure out for himself what to do about underwear.

Clothes in hand, I took one last look around the too-still room. Then I headed out to my brother's car, where the open road, Kyra Kelley, and his drunk ex–best friend were waiting.

4

There was one thing I had to do first.

When I pulled into the lot of Reagan County Park, I was relieved to find it empty. Certain allowances usually seem to be made for grieving people, but this probably wouldn't be one of them. I turned the car off and glanced over at Rusty, who was passed out, head back, mouth open, in the front seat. He didn't flinch when I got out and slammed my door or when I went around to each of the back doors and rolled the windows all the way down so he didn't stink up the car. After another look around to make sure no one was watching, I walked across the dewy grass to where the town emblem, the Santa Rita No. 1, stood proudly, cordoned off by thick, twisted ropes stiff with dirt and age.

The story of the blessed oil derrick was Finn's favorite to listen to as a kid and our dad's favorite to tell. Dad had a knack for weaving words together that made it seem just as exciting every time he told it. According to him, the Santa Rita No. 1 was Big Lake's very own miracle. It was one of the first oil derricks built here, and after twenty-one long months of construction and several more of dry, hopeless prospecting, it didn't look very promising.

But one spring day, a partner in the local oil venture climbed to the top of it with a single dried rose in his hand. His name was Frank Pickrell, and he'd received the rose from a group of Catholic women investors all the way in New York. With every oil-less day that passed, they'd gotten more and more nervous about their investment, so they decided to take matters into their own hands. They had a priest bless the rose in the name of Saint Rita, the patron saint of the impossible, and they'd instructed Pickrell to scatter its dried petals over the top of the oil derrick as a sort of christening. Pickrell was willing to try anything by then, so he did just what they said. He climbed to the top of the rig and let the crushed red petals swirl in the wind and flutter down over the greased iron and cracked ground. The very next day, the rig spouted her first gusher, spraying the countryside with shiny black hope and securing the town's future in oil.

We didn't grow up religious, and there weren't many things Finn wasn't confident about, but when he was up against one of them, he always came and grabbed a pinch of the Santa Rita's dirt for good luck. If it was a game he needed it for, he'd smear it on the inside of his helmet. If there was a girl he wasn't sure would say yes, he'd rub a few specks between his hands before he asked her out. And it never let him down. He believed in the patron saint of the impossible.

It was kind of a joke between the two of us, but this morning I figured if there ever was a time I needed her, it was now. I pulled Finn's letter out of my purse and held the envelope open with one hand while I bent for a pinch of the blessed dirt with the other. Slowly, I rubbed my fingers together above the open envelope until the last tiny specks fell over the pages that contained his words and wishes.

Now I could go.

When I stood again, I felt a little glimmer of something in me. Hope, or confidence maybe, that I was doing the right thing. That I wasn't completely crazy. That Finn would be proud and the impossible would become possible. I nodded a grateful thank-you to the Santa Rita and headed back to the car.

The engine rumbled when I laid my foot into the gas, and dry August air whipped through the open windows, blowing my hair into tangles all around me. Rusty slumped against the passenger door, snoring and down for the count, and I prayed he'd stay that way for a while. I needed to be alone with the road in front of me. And with Kyra Kelley, who was singing about wishing she'd never had to grow up. I understood, more so now than I had when I bought the album.

My whole life, I'd set my course by Finn, depending on him to guide me, like old sailors did with the stars. He'd been the one with the big ideas and the force of will to see them through, but now it was supposed to be me. Without him. The thought was foreign and hard to swallow. Even so, I told myself that the miles of desert and nothing towns stretched out in front of me were full with the possibility to do it. It didn't matter that I only half believed it.

Rusty shifted in the seat and took in the deep, heavy breath of someone who was worlds away from consciousness. With him like that, I could almost pretend like it wasn't a terrible idea to bring him along. He did, at one time, have his good points. Ever since I could remember, he'd been Finn's most loyal and devoted friend. They were inseparable, despite that they were so different, and Rusty spent more time at our house growing up than his. Which I understood.

At his house, it was just him and his dad, who drank too much and blamed Rusty for the way his life had turned out. In his sober moments, which were few, he obsessed over Rusty's football playing and was the proudest dad ever, convinced his boy was going to the pros. Inevitably, though, when game nights rolled around, he'd show up to the stands already primed up, and I'd hope the boys played well, especially Rusty, so his dad wouldn't make a scene. Sometimes it was the other team or the coach or the refs that were the target, but most often it was Rusty—something he didn't do well enough or fast enough or hard enough.

So he came to our house, where Gina would make us big dinners, fawn over the boys, and do her best to smooth it all over. They went out a lot too, especially by their senior year. After the game, they'd leave the house all showered up and smelling like Old Spice and mint gum, and roll off into the night in the Impala, leaving me behind wondering what went on out at the Pit or the field or whatever party spot they were headed to. I never got to go with them no matter how much I begged, but the following Monday at school, I'd always hear stories about the parties they'd been at. They *were* the party. Finn because of his friendly, contagious personality that could make you like him in five seconds flat, and Rusty because of his football bravado and ability to shotgun a beer faster than anyone around.

They were a team, on and off the field, so it wasn't surprising when Northern Arizona University recruited both of them with full rides and they accepted. The only surprise came right before graduation, when—out of nowhere—Finn turned his scholarship down and enlisted, and Rusty turned on the both of us so fast, it was like they'd never been friends to begin with. With Rusty passing us by without so much as a glance and Finn getting ready for boot camp instead of college, nothing could have been more surprising or more wrong. Until now.

I pushed the thought away and set my eyes on the horizon. Between the heat of the day and the heat seeping through the floorboards from the engine, my feet were burning inside the boots I'd pulled on without thinking, so I took a gulp of water that had now turned warm and worked on slipping them off while driving. The left one wasn't so hard. I just had to dig the heel into the floor and slide my foot out. The relief was immediate, but so was the smell of leather and foot sweat. I glanced over at Rusty and inched the window down the last bit. My gas-pedal foot was trickier. I moved it off to the side and put my bare toes on the pedal so both feet were on it, then I gingerly lifted my booted foot and used one hand to yank it off.

The car swerved, and I overcorrected, tossing Rusty into the door. "What the hell?" He sat up rubbing his head and looked around, trying to get his bearings. "What happened?" He didn't wait for me to answer, but sniffed. "Ugh. Didn't anyone ever teach you to wear socks?"

I looked at him out the corner of my eye, being careful to keep the car steady, and turned the music down. He leaned his head toward the open window. "You got any aspirin?"

"Nope," I said. And I was glad.

"Water?"

I glanced down at the almost-empty bottle in the cup holder next to me and motioned at it. "That's it, right there." He grabbed it without waiting for my permission and swallowed the last sip.

"I didn't say you could drink it. That was supposed to last me until the next stop."

He rolled his eyes, then rubbed his forehead. "I'll buy you a new one when we get there."

I sighed and popped in a piece of gum, then threw one at him. "Here. Your breath stinks."

He unwrapped it, bent it into his mouth, then leaned his head toward the window again, eyes closed, chewing slowly. "Your feet stink."

"You're smelling yourself." He didn't say anything. "What were you drinking, anyway? You're sweatin' it." I tucked my free foot beneath the seat. He grimaced and slung one arm over his face, dismissing the question.

Yep. Bringing him had been a horrible idea. I reached for the tape deck and turned the volume up full, determined to drown out anything else he had to say, and it was perfect that Kyra was singing a song about a no-good, small-town guy who was just plain mean. I couldn't have cued it up better myself.

Rusty lifted his arm off his face and gave me exactly the kind of look I'd expected. I was satisfied for less than a second before he leaned forward and hit the eject button and yanked out the cassette adapter. He held it up, my iPod dangling like it was some sacrilegious thing, and I grabbed for it.

"Hey—"

He shook it. "An *iPod*? This is a 1967 Chevy Impala. Are you f'in kiddin' me?"

I flinched as he wrapped the cord around it and stashed it in the glove box, shaking his head at my disregard for the old rules. I knew what he was gonna say before he said it. Somewhere along the line, he and Finn had decided that the only music that could be played in the car was classic rock. The kind they turned up and sang along to and that I associated with people my aunt's age but was probably even older than that. Secretly, I liked a few of the songs, but I never would have admitted it.

"Never do that again." Rusty leaned forward and found their old radio station immediately, which I was surprised at, since we were almost to the New Mexico state line. He turned it up louder than I'd had it, and I recognized the song. I could feel him looking over at me, grinning like he'd just put me in my place. I rolled my eyes, but for just a second it felt like a flash of old times.

After an uninterrupted triple play of REO Speedwagon, we pulled in to a gas station that looked like something out of one of those movies where some old creep with missing teeth is behind the counter waiting for an unsuspecting customer to walk in. I yanked my boots on and ran around the side, to where I'd seen a bathroom sign. When I got back, Rusty was standing next to the gas pump, gulping down water from a gallon container. He set it down on the trunk with a thud, then popped open a bottle of aspirin and threw a few in his mouth, not bothering with any water to swallow them. I came around to the pump.

"Did you pay for the gas?"

"Yeah." He still looked like hell, but I could tell from his eyes he was sobering up.

"Thanks," I said, then stood there awkwardly for a second when he didn't answer. "I'm gonna get some candy or something. You want anything else?"

He shook his head as he pulled the nozzle out of the tank and shut it. "Nope. I need to sleep this shit off." Without another word, he screwed the gas cap back on, walked around to his side of the car, and got in. Charming.

A set of bells jangled on the door when I pushed it open, and a loud fan blew a cloud of cigarette smoke and perfume right at me. "Hi there," a girl's voice said from behind the counter. She was a few years older than me, and pretty—honey-colored hair, blue eyes, thick black eyeliner. The kind of girl Rusty'd probably hit on as soon as he walked in. Nowhere near the toothless old guy I'd been picturing. "Your fella out there's in a bad way." She laughed. "Still pretty cute, though." I didn't know quite how to respond, and it must have shown. She smiled. "Sorry. I get bored is all. You two are the most interesting thing that's happened all day."

I glanced around the tiny store, hoping for a candy rack. "I'll bet." She popped her gum and went back to her magazine, and I found what I wanted. I went ahead and grabbed a couple of bags of Sour Skittles, a pack of gum, and a box of Red Vines, because that's what Finn always bought at pit stops. On the way up to the counter, I stopped in front of a display of little tree-shaped air fresheners. I preferred vanilla, but Finn loved the irony of driving around in the Impala with new car scent hanging from the dash, so I added the familiar blue tree to my haul and smiled. When I took it all up to the counter, the girl at the register set her magazine down, open to a full-page collage of pictures, all of Kyra Kelley.

"Oh, wow, can I see this?" She nodded, and I spun the magazine around so it was facing me.

She nodded as she punched the keys and popped her gum. "Just got it in the mail today. Her first interview in a long time, all about how she's giving everything up. Walkin' away, just like that. Crazy, you know?"

I looked at the shots, mostly candid, by paparazzi. Her walking out of a Starbucks, Frappuccino in hand, her going into a sushi restaurant, her in workout clothes and huge sunglasses, carrying a bottle of water. Her in the backyard of her newly purchased home, somewhere "away from the generic luxury of the Hollywood Hills" and closer to family—her words.

"Yeah," I said absently. "I do." I looked around for the magazine rack. "Got any more copies of this?" There were no magazines in the store.

"Nah, it's mine. But I've read it five times already. Take it." She grabbed it and slid it into the brown bag with my candy.

"Really? Thank you . . . I . . . thanks!"

She smiled. "No problem. Thank *you* for dropping by with your hot, hungover boyfriend. You two have a nice trip."

The bells jangled again as I pushed through the door, flipping to a full-page photo of Kyra Kelley on stage, wearing a smile that was all hope and light. It didn't matter that Rusty was leaned back against the seat, passed out again, when I opened the door. I was ecstatic. I had something to go on.

"Rusty! Wake up. The girl inside just gave me this magazine, and it shows Kyra's new house and talks about her last show and *everything*." He mumbled something unintelligible, and I got in. "You don't understand what this means." He didn't answer, but I didn't care.

It felt like some sort of sign that what I was doing was right and not crazy. I slid the magazine into my purse next to Finn's letter, tied the little blue tree to one of the AC vents, and revved the engine, ready to drive for three days straight if that's what it took to get to Kyra Kelley's last show.

5

Somewhere past the New Mexico state line, after two bags of Sour Skittles and endless miles of static and dusty interstate, I lost momentum. With no working clock, I had no idea what time it was, and my purse with my phone in it was too far away to reach. Rusty was snoring away, just as he had been for the last few hours and was of no use to me. I shifted my weight in the seat, stretched out my left leg, and leaned forward on the steering wheel, then pinched my damp sundress away from my back. It had to be near five, but it was still at least ninety-five degrees out. And it was becoming painfully clear how much I hadn't thought through—driving through the desert in August with no AC, no real plan, and Rusty as a companion. Not to mention only four days to get from Texas to California and back to Austin—all before my first class. I was pushing it.

I strained to see down the road, hoping for a billboard or another mileage sign to the next town. Anything. I hadn't been paying close attention to where we were because according to the map I'd looked at, we'd be on the 40 forever. The landscape had changed gradually since we'd crossed the border. Flat farmland had given way to barren, rocky desert that was pretty in its own sort of way, with the cloudless blue sky and surprisingly fresh smell of heat and dirt. Still, I had no idea where we were or how close we might be to somewhere decent to stop. Or where we would sleep. If Rusty could get it together, we could take shifts driving through the night and not have to worry about that at all.

I nudged him, gently at first. "Hey. Wake up. I need you to look at the map for me." He licked his lips and furrowed his brow, but his eyes stayed closed. I tried again, this time with a well-aimed fist in his shoulder. "Rusty. Wake *up*."

It worked. He sat up and yawned loudly, rubbed the heels of his hands into his eyes, then squinted over at me, one eye still half-closed. "What time is it?" His voice was gravelly from sleep, and he went straight for the water at his feet.

"I don't know. Check my phone. I can't reach my purse." I motioned at it down by his feet, and he grabbed it, rummaging through roughly until he held my phone.

"Almost six, and you got eight missed calls," he said, dropping it back in. He looked around. "Where the hell are we?"

"Somewhere in New Mexico." I grabbed the map from beneath the seat and did my best to ignore the guilt creeping over me about lying to Gina and not returning Lilah's calls. "Here," I said, shoving the map at him.

He looked at it blankly. "That's not gonna help us if you don't know where we are."

"I know where we are." I paused, looked around for some point of reference to avoid looking stupid. "We're on Highway 40, headed west . . ." Lucky for me, the outline of a sign came into view, just up the road. ". . . coming into . . . Santa Rosa, the City of Natural Lakes. Eight miles. See? Look it up." I pushed the map at him, but he didn't open it.

"So let's stop in Santa Rosa. Bet they got a place to eat."

I didn't want to stop now that he'd been the one to suggest it, but my stomach felt hollow, and stretching my legs outside the car would feel like heaven, so I put my foot down hard on the gas, and we covered the eight miles in less than five minutes. The Pala was practically older than me and Finn and Rusty combined, but it was fast. Finn had made sure of that.

We pulled into the Comet II Drive-In, which looked like it had probably been around since the old Route 66 days. Though it was styled like an old-fashioned burger joint, it boasted "The Best Mexican Food in Town," which was good enough for me. After I'd ordered half the menu, the girl at the pickup window seemed surprised to see only two of us in the car. I motioned at Rusty and fake whispered. "He's hungover. Needs the grease." She bent down so she could see in the car, and Rusty gave her a nod, sending a flush up her neck that bloomed in her cheeks.

"Y'all have a good night. And good luck with that hangover." She winked at Rusty, who smiled back, knowing exactly the effect he'd had on her. Gag. I pulled out of the drive-thru before he could say anything back, and plunged my hand into the grease-dotted bag of tortilla chips.

He watched me, amused. "You never were one to eat ladylike."

I crunched a too-hot, perfectly salty chip in my mouth and glanced over. "I've been driving for half the day without anything to eat." I swallowed and reached for my soda. "You were passed out, remember?" I took a long gulp before I said anything worse.

Rusty reached in for a few chips. "Yeah, I know. I feel like crap."

I swallowed another mouthful of chips and looked around for a good spot. We were rolling slowly down the main street of the town, and I took in what I could in the dimming light. It was a modern little desert city with bits of fifties-era nostalgia all over the place. We passed the city hall, the Route 66 Auto Museum, and more than one Mexican cantina.

Rusty motioned out the window with his head. "Sign says there's a campground that way. We could pull into a spot to eat."

I made the turn, and we followed the carved wooden signs that eventually ended at an empty kiosk with sign-in instructions. Since we wouldn't be staying the night, I didn't bother with any of it, but I hoped there'd be an empty spot to rest in for a little while.

Once I rounded the first turn, I realized we were gonna be lucky if we found one. The campground was full with the last of the summer's campers spilling from one spot into the next. The unmistakable smell of campfire and barbecue drifted on the evening breeze, along with the sounds of laughter and kids running wild. I let the car coast down the camp road. Three boys, probably eight or so, zoomed by on their bikes, yelling after each other. Just before they ducked down a dirt path, one of them turned around and yelled, "Nice car!" I smiled. The whole place had that summer evening calm, the kind where no one's worried about anything except enjoying it.

Rusty pointed. "Looks empty over there." I saw the spot he meant, and when I pulled up to it, he leaned out to check the wooden post. "Must be your lucky day."

"Yeah, right." I pulled in and shut off the car, listening for a second to the bubbling of the radiator water mingle with the other sounds of the evening. Together, they gave off the feeling that everything was winding down for the night. I was, and I figured maybe it wouldn't be so bad to stay after all. We could sleep in the Pala and leave first thing in the morning.

Rusty was already out of the car stretching and, from the looks of it, feeling a little better. He grabbed our food and set it on the wooden picnic table, then sat next to it with his signature wide grin spread out across his face. "Sure as hell didn't see myself ending up here today."

I pushed the door open with my shoulder and got out, arms and legs stretching almost like a reflex. "I didn't see you ending up here either." He nodded but didn't say anything. I sat on the other side of the table and picked up a burrito. "You were kind of an ass earlier."

He put his elbows on his knees. "Yeah," he said, nodding at the ground. "I was."

We were silent, which could have been awkward except that just at that moment, a guy in board shorts, a T-shirt, and flip-flops tromped through the shrubs separating our campsite from his. He walked to the back corner of our site, completely oblivious that we were sitting ten feet from him. He started to untie his shorts, and I wasn't sure what he was doing until he turned his back to us, planted his feet apart, and started to pee. Rusty cleared his throat.

The kid turned casually over his shoulder, midstream, and smiled apologetically. "Oh, dude, sorry, guys. Thought it was empty over here still." He craned his neck a bit more, and his eyes caught mine. "Oh." He smiled. "Hi there."

He turned back to the job at hand, and Rusty nudged me. "He's hittin' on you while he's taking a piss."

Still relieving himself, the guy yelled over his shoulder. "I'm MULTITASKING!" He finished up, swayed a little, and tied his shorts before turning toward the bushes he'd come from.

"Hey! We gotta find a new place to piss!"

Muffled laughter drifted over. "Why? You flood it or somethin'? You've been pissin' every five minutes since you opened your first beer!"

He looked over at us. Grinned at me so big, his eyes closed. "Nah. There's . . . a girl over here." Rusty nudged me again, this time stifling a laugh.

Another yell came from the other side. "Is she hot?"

The kid put his hands to his mouth and yelled up to the sky. "Superhot!" Then he turned and gave me a whaddya-gonna-do shrug. "It's true. You are." I felt my cheeks flush and sipped on my Coke. He was close to my age, maybe a little younger, and a little part of me liked that he was hitting on me in front of Rusty.

He sauntered over to us and stuck out his hand, swaying a bit. "Name's Wyatt."

Rusty just looked at him for a second before he spoke.

"You were just pissing two seconds ago. I'm eating. I'm not gonna shake your hand."

Both were quiet a minute before I cracked up. I'd been thinking it but didn't want to be rude. Rusty didn't seem to mind about that, and judging by the smile of understanding that now crossed Wyatt's face, he didn't either.

"Aw, geez. My bad. Sorry about pissin' in your campsite." His eyes flicked to me, and I thought I saw a hint of embarrassment. Which was cute. *He* was cute, in a funny, earnest kind of way. "We got a lot of beers. Come have some. We'll find a new campsite to piss in."

Before I could answer, Rusty cut in. "Yeah, sure. I could use a cold one, just as soon as we finish eatin'."

Wyatt smiled and put a heavy hand on Rusty's shoulder. "Can I ask you a question?"

Rusty nodded, mouth full of burrito. "Shoot."

Wyatt leaned in to him and pointed at me, like he was being secretive, then whispered loud enough for me to hear. "She's, like, your sister or something, right?"

Rusty took a drink from his soda and smiled. "Nope. Not my sister. Thanks for askin', though." I rolled my eyes. He was enjoying this.

Wyatt's shoulders slumped a bit, and I tried to hide my smile. "Just checkin', bro." He turned to go. "Well. You guys cruise on over when you're done, anyway. We got beers. Lots of 'em."

"Will do." Rusty patted him on the shoulder. "And hey. She's not my girl either—just my friend's little sister."

Wyatt's smile returned, and he fixed his brown eyes on me. "In that case, what's *your* name?" He smiled lazily, waiting for me to finish chewing, and I decided he was cute enough to humor him. I swallowed, then looked right at him. "Honor."

He rested against the picnic table next to me and made no effort to keep from leaning into me. "Honor . . ." He said it with great reverence, then pursed his lips together a second. I figured he was about to ask me where the name came from, or make a guess at it, because that's what most people did when I first met them. Instead, he looked me over, beginning with my face, made it all the way down to my feet, and paused, almost imperceptibly, at my chest on his way back up to my eyes. And then he said, with complete seriousness, "I like your boots."

A mouthful of soda erupted from Rusty's mouth. I looked at Wyatt, completely speechless, not knowing whether to laugh or slap him. It was a good line, especially because they did happen to be my favorite boots.

Wyatt was unfazed when he pushed off the table and looked to Rusty. "Beer's over there. Come when you're done." Then he pointed to me with a grin. "You too, boots." With that he turned and did his swagger-stagger back to his pass-through. Just before he ducked through the bushes, he looked back at us and grinned another drunken grin. "Superhot."

Then he was gone.

I looked over at Rusty, who had composed himself and was now wiping the soda off his jeans. After a second, we both burst out laughing. And we kept going, probably for longer than it warranted, but it felt good to laugh. It was the first time I really had in the two weeks since I'd heard about Finn. And it was the first point in the day that felt like, just maybe, life could find a new normal.

After a minute I leaned back, elbows on the table, and looked up for the twinkle of the first star in the evening sky. When we were little, it was a ritual Finn and I did on the front porch. He'd make his wish silently, and I would too, but I never could keep a secret; and I'd tell him what I wished every time. He'd always tell me it wouldn't come true if I told, but I didn't believe him. I'd had plenty of them come true, from a new box of crayons showing up out of nowhere to a bag of candy left on my bed. It had been a while, though, and the only thing I'd wish for now was impossible. I found the first star in a patch of burnt-orange sky, above the crinkly purple mountains in the distance, and then I wished my brother back anyway.

Rusty leaned back next to me and sighed. "I'm sorry, H, about earlier. I—"

"Don't worry about it. Finn probably would have wanted you along anyway. . . ." I let my words drift off. I didn't want to talk about him right now, and I got the feeling Rusty didn't either, so I sat up. "So. You think that guy was drunk?"

"Hope so." Rusty sat back up. "Good line about the boots, though. Too bad he has no idea how bad your feet stink under those things."

I smacked him on the thigh. "You really are an ass." But it was true, and I had to laugh. "Just don't tell him, or it'll ruin my superhotness."

We finished up our fast-food Mexican feast, crumpled the greasy yellow papers, and stretched our legs again. By the time we headed to the trail between the campsites, the sky had deepened to indigo dotted with glittering stars. A thin layer of campfire smoke hung above us, creating just enough haze to soften the night sky, and I paused a moment to soak in the serenity of it all before I ducked my head through the bushes.

Wyatt was the first one I saw standing beside the crackling campfire. His face lit up, and he stumbled a few steps toward me. "It's my dream girl." He offered his hand again, and this time I obliged with my own. He took it lightly and led me toward his friends, smiling back at me instead of looking where he was going. I opened my mouth to warn him about the rocks bordering the fire, but he tripped over them and pitched backward. I yanked hard on his hand, and at the last second he caught himself. Then he looked at me with another wry grin. "For you I would burn."

I couldn't not laugh. Even if his lines were cheesy, his eyes were warm and sincere, and it was nice to be flirted with. As Rusty ducked through the bushes behind me, Wyatt raised an eyebrow at him. Then he turned to the guy and girl sitting in lawn chairs around the fire and said, "So you all know, she's just his friend's little sister." He winked at me, then sat-fell back into his own chair by the fire and picked up a beer.

The girl stood and came over to me, smiling apologetically. "Sorry about Wyatt. He's kind of a lightweight. Two beers and he becomes the world's biggest dumbass." She stuck out her hand and I shook it. "I'm Corrie." She gestured at the guy who was still sitting by the fire. "And that's Sam, Wyatt's older brother."

I nodded at them, well aware of the clench of my jaw at the word "brother." Rusty stepped up next to me and shook Corrie's hand, smiling his good ol' boy smile. "Rusty. And this is Honor." I watched her for the little flutter effect he had on most girls when he put in any effort. She wasn't his usual type, but she was definitely good looking. Wavy brown hair, tan skin, and sleepy hazel eyes like you see on lingerie models. She smiled in a friendly way, but not overly so, and I guessed Sam was probably her boyfriend.

As if on cue, Sam stood and smiled a more-sober version of Wyatt's smile. "Nice to meet you guys." He put a relaxed arm around Corrie's shoulders and nodded at the cooler. "You want a beer?"

Rusty didn't miss a beat. "Don't mind if I do."

Sam looked to me. I didn't particularly *like* beer, but I learned in my brief high school party career that a girl who would drink a beer was a heck of a lot cooler than one who wouldn't. "Sure." I smiled. "Thanks."

While he went to get them, Corrie pulled two more lawn chairs out of the truck, and Rusty and I brought them over to the fire ring. Sam returned with an armful of dripping-cold beers, tossed one to Rusty, and handed Corrie and me each one but didn't bother with Wyatt, who was leaning back in his chair, humming softly to himself. When I set my chair next to him, he winked at me. Corrie walked around behind him to her chair, ruffling his hair. "Keep tryin', Don Juan."

She sat on the other side of me and twisted the cap off her beer. "Ignore him. He's got a thing for girls in boots and dresses. Spent the entire trip trying to convince us to drive all the way down to Texas for that." She nodded at my feet and smiled. "Those are cute, by the way. I like the red."

I took a drink and was surprised at how not-bad the beer tasted. The iciness of it was a good complement to the still-hot evening, and it put me a little more at ease. "Thanks." I laughed a little. "Guess I fit the stereotype, then. That's where we're from."

"Hear that, Wyatt? Your dream girl's from Texas." She reached around and poked him.

He sat forward in his chair and smiled, then leaned across me and wagged a finger at Corrie. "I told you they know how to dress there." He turned to me, forearms resting on my legs, and I sat back slightly, all too conscious of our close proximity. Wyatt didn't notice. He smiled so big, his eyes closed, then pushed himself back up and raised his beer. "So. To girls from Texas, who wear boots with dresses." Nobody else heard the toast, but I clinked my bottle with his and took a sip, surprised at how good it felt to be just a girl in a dress, instead of one wrapped up tight in grief.

6

"So, what're you guys doin' over this way?"

Sam had no way to know that when he turned to Rusty, his question snapped me out of my slight buzz and sent me into silent panic. It was a normal enough question.

I watched Rusty. *Please, don't say it. Don't tell him about Finn or Kyra Kelley or anything.* He glanced at me and casually drank from his beer, allowing me to answer. I silently thanked him. You never knew what might come out of his mouth, but at least he realized the last thing I wanted was to explain what we were doing there.

I kept it vague and casual. "Just a road trip." When I said it, its unspoken meaning tugged at the edges of my composure. Really, it was hard to believe what I was doing—that the day after my brother's funeral, I was on my way to California for a concert, sitting around a campfire drinking with strangers.

And Rusty. From the moment I'd found out about Finn, nothing felt real. This didn't either, which made me wonder if that's how it would be from here on out—if I'd always feel so lost. But Finn's letter had given me something to hold on to in the midst of it all, and I wasn't about to let go now.

Since Rusty had told Wyatt I was his friend's little sister, the next logical question would be to ask where my brother was, so I steered us away from that one quick. "How 'bout y'all? What are you here for?" Nobody else seemed to notice the change in my tone of voice, but Rusty's eyes flicked over to me, and I wondered what he thought of my not mentioning Finn. It felt wrong to me, but I didn't want to hear it. Especially from him.

Wyatt laughed like I'd said something funny, and Sam chuckled before he answered. "We're here for the scuba diving, of course."

I didn't know if he was kidding, and my expression must've said so, because Wyatt turned to me, once again mock serious. "You think he's joking. He's not. Corrie here dragged us all the way down here to scuba dive in the middle of the desert. We live in *California*, for cryin' out loud. At the beach."

Corrie nodded like she'd been hearing it all the way from California, then smiled good naturedly. "Yes, but we don't have a blue hole in California that you can see the stars from the bottom of, through eighty feet of water." She shrugged. "Besides. It's an adventure, and you guys are always talking about how you need to have more of those." She turned to me. "I read about it in a magazine. It's called a cenote, which is like an underground cave but filled with water. There's a spring at the bottom of it that keeps it filled with the clearest water you've ever seen. And it's warm all year round."

Sam leaned over and patted her leg. "So her plan is for us to get up while it's still dark, dive down so we can see the stars, then watch the sun come up. From the bottom of the Blue Hole."

Rusty raised his eyebrows, impressed. "Nice."

I didn't say anything, but I flashed on a line from Finn's letter: *Watch the stars disappear*, and I looked up at the sky, almost waiting for a reaction.

Corrie gave a nod, finished off her beer, and stood. "Anyone want another?" I'd barely gotten halfway through mine, but the boys raised their hands, so she went to the cooler and returned with another dripping round.

Wyatt laid his hand on the arm of my chair. "So," he said, bringing me back to the moment. "You should dive with us."

"Did you miss the part where I'm from Texas? We don't scuba dive there."

"Know how to swim?"

"Yes."

Wyatt furrowed his brow, like he was thinking. Then the idea came to him. "I could breathe for you."

I briefly pictured us locked together beneath the water. "Like mouth to *mouth*?" He had to be joking.

He laughed and raised an eyebrow. "I could do that, too, if you want, but no. What I meant was, we could put an extra hose on my tank that you could breathe from, give you a weight belt, and have you dive with me so you can watch the sun rise."

It sounded amazing and beautiful and scary all at the same time and was exactly the type of thing Finn would have done without hesitation. Would have convinced me to do too. I glanced across the fire at Rusty, who was watching me with a smirk that made me wonder how many beers he'd had. He didn't say anything, but he didn't look away either.

Corrie bumped my shoulder. "You should, Honor. It'll be gorgeous. When else are you gonna get a chance like this? And it's not complicated. I can walk you through it, but basically you just have to relax and breathe." She smiled with the warmth of a good friend, and out of nowhere I missed Lilah. If I'd opened the letter earlier, she'd be the one next to me in the passenger seat. We'd listen to Kyra Kelley the whole way and snap pictures of each other with the wind in our hair. But she was on her way to school, thinking I was too, with no idea about any of this.

Sam interrupted my thoughts. "Corrie's a good teacher. You'll be in great hands."

Wyatt tipped his head to touch mine and held out his hands in the firelight. "These ones are pretty good too."

I took one of his hands in my own and examined it. "I guess they are. As long as you wash them after you pee."

He pulled it back and smiled into his lap. "I'm not gonna live that one down, am I?"

"Not a chance. But I'm in. I'll try it." It came out more confident than I felt, but they were right about having a chance like this. Finn would've said so too.

Corrie clapped her hands, Wyatt nodded, satisfied, and Sam stood to wedge another log into the orange-hot coals. "Rusty, you in too? We've got enough gear."

"Yeah, maybe so." He shrugged. "If we stay the night." His eyes met mine for a brief second, and I saw in them . . . what? Disapproval? Jealousy? *What?*

Two more logs on the fire and a case of empty beer bottles later, we were most definitely staying. The camp sounds of kids playing and adults talking and clanking pots and pans had died down and given way to the kind of calm that makes you want to speak softly. An occasional pair of flashlights floated by on the road as campers made their way to the restroom, and we sat within the orangey glow of the campfire.

Corrie and Sam had pulled their chairs close, and she slung her long legs over his lap. They tipped their heads way back, laughing at themselves and trying to pick out constellations from the stars spread thick in the sky. Sam pointed. "I know that's something right . . . there. You see that thing that looks kind of like a cross?" Corrie sat up and moved her head closer to his squinting to see what he was talking about.

Wyatt and I had our heads leaned back on the now-cool metal chair frames, eyes to the sky. You could make any number of crosses with the myriad of stars dotting the sky above us. All around us, really. Aside from the shrubs dividing the campsites, nothing else obstructed the view, which gave the feeling we were under a dome made of tiny glittering lights.

Rusty's voice surprised me. "It's Cygnus." I'd thought he'd fallen asleep in his chair a while ago. While the rest of us switched to water so we could wake up at 'dark thirty' for our scuba dive, he'd kept on, getting quieter with each beer, while we compared everything we could about Texas and California.

"It's *what*?" I wasn't even sure he'd said a real word, and I was so tired, I didn't want to put in the energy to figure it out. I didn't move, but kept looking for a cross.

"Sig. Nus. It's a swan, not a cross."

Sam jabbed a finger at the sky. "That's it! That's the one! Cygnus. I've heard it called the Northern Cross, too, though."

I sat up in time to see Rusty tip his bottle back, swallow hard, then nod. "Yeah, that too. Cygnus is the name of the swan." I didn't know what was more surprising: that he figured out where Sam was pointing or that he knew the proper name of the constellation.

Corrie kept her head back, still looking. "Is there a story about it? I always used to love the stories about how people or the gods or whatever became stars."

It was quiet a moment as we all pondered a possible story for the cross/swan. It was Rusty, again, who spoke. "Yeah, there's a story." I waited for the smart-ass line that had to be coming. His way of giving Sam and Corrie a hard time. Instead, he sat forward in his chair, elbows resting on his thighs.

"There were a couple of buddies, guys who woulda done anything for each other. And they always liked to one-up the other doing wild shit. So one of 'em came up with the idea to race their chariot things across the sky, around the sun, and back again." He paused, and I caught a shift in his tone. The others were still looking up at the stars, listening to his story like kids getting tucked in. I watched Rusty. He twirled his empty beer bottle in the dirt in front of him, then continued without looking up. "So one of the guys crashed his cart and ended up stuck at the bottom of this river. And his buddy, Cygnus, saw it and dove down to get him, but the guy was all tangled up in the weeds at the bottom. Well Cygnus dove down again and again, trying to get his friend loose, but he couldn't do it no matter how hard he tried. So he finally gave up and sat down on the bank of the river and begged Zeus to do something 'cuz he knew his best friend was gone."

He paused, and I knew the others were silently waiting to hear the end of the story. I couldn't have said anything if I wanted to. In that moment, his words sat on my chest, heavy with something I could feel but didn't wholly understand. Something that hurt in a more real way than anything else had in the last few days. Something the two of us, sitting there, shared.

He looked up and held my eyes as he started again slowly. "So Zeus took pity on this guy, Cygnus, because he was so broken up about his friend. And he made him a deal: He told him that if he turned him into a swan, he'd be able to dive down and get his friend. So he could have a proper burial and be sent off to wherever in peace. The catch was, he'd have to give up his immortality to do it. And stay a swan until he died." He paused and I looked up at the sky, hoping no one could see how hard I was working to hold back what felt like a warm flood rising behind my eyes.

Rusty went on. "Cygnus didn't give it a second thought. Traded his life to honor his friend. And then when he died, Zeus stuck him up in the sky as a swan for being such a stand-up guy." He gave the beer bottle another spin, and when it got away from him, he didn't bother to grab for it. "Anyway, that's the story of that one."

I stared up at the four stars that were Cygnus, and couldn't help but picture Rusty and Finn, wild and inseparable. When they hit the field together, they may as well have been racing chariots across the sky. They were all fire and glory when they played. People called them the dream team and did stories and news features about the best friends who were also the best pair of cornerbacks in Texas high school football. There was no such thing as one without the other.

For the first time since Finn's death, I was sad for someone besides myself.

More than a few beats passed before Corrie sat up. "Aww, I like that one. Sad, though. How do you know it? No offense, but you don't seem like the astronomy type." She smiled and we all turned, waiting for his answer. I knew, though. My brother was the astronomy type.

Rusty turned his head to the side and spit. "Heard it from a friend." He stood. "I gotta take a piss." To anyone else, he probably just sounded drunk, but I recognized the edge in his voice. I watched him disappear into the dark and wondered for a second if I should follow or try to talk to him about Finn, but I didn't have it in me. Instead, I wiped my damp cheeks as discreetly as I could and sat up in my chair.

Corrie stood and stretched, looking at Sam. "I'm going to bed. You coming?"

"Yep." He checked the coals in the fire pit. "You guys can just let that burn down if you're gonna be up a little while."

We nodded, and Sam put his hands on Corrie's shoulders, steering her to their tent. "Wyatt, you're in the truck tonight. See you before sunrise."

When they were zipped into their tent, Wyatt stretched his arms over his head and sighed. "I gotta learn a few of those stories about the stars. You seemed pretty impressed over there."

I kept my eyes on the fire. "What do you mean?"

He looked at me with a puzzled kind of sympathy. "You

got all teary eyed. It was cute." He put his arm around my shoulders and pulled me gently into him. "See, it's perfect, because then you need someone to cheer you up." His arm around me felt good, and I smiled but didn't say anything. Just let myself lean into him the slightest bit. He was warm and smelled like campfire smoke, and I rested my head on his shoulder the way you do with someone close to you.

"Easy there, bro. She's got a marine for a brother."

My breath caught in my throat, and I sat up lightning quick, despite the immediate sinking feeling in my chest. Wyatt laughed and raised his hands in surrender as Rusty walked over slowly from the dark to the now-dim circle of firelight. He was smiling a smile that put me on edge instantly. *Don't,* I begged silently. *Don't say anything else.*

Casually, he kicked a pebble in front of him. "Yeah, if her brother saw some guy she'd just met with his arms around her, he'd put a boot in his ass." He turned his eyes on me. "Ain't that right, H?"

I didn't know what to say. The sympathy I'd felt for him a few minutes earlier went icy. I stared at him and hoped he could see it. *Stop it.*

Wyatt spoke up. "No worries, man. We were just talking."

Rusty considered this, then sat down in the chair on the other side of Wyatt. Put a hand on his shoulder. "Good. Because her brother ain't around anymore."

Hot, angry tears pooled at the corners of my eyes, and I sat, paralyzed. Wyatt looked over at me, confused. Rusty let go of him and sat back in his chair, shaking his head. "Nope. He ain't around anymore, because he thought it'd be a good idea to sign up for the marines instead of playing football, and then he went and got himself blown up, probably for no reason at all."

"Rusty, *stop*." I barely got it out. The anger in his voice had made my own shaky.

He glanced at me, then back to the fire pit. "They put him in the ground yesterday, and now here we are." He laughed bitterly. "What are we doing here again, Honor? Going to a *concert*? The day after his funeral?"

"Shut up, Rusty." I stood and wiped my eyes, and now there was no controlling my voice. Tears spilled over, down my cheeks, and I spat my words at him. "Shut the hell up!"

Wyatt pushed his chair back slowly and stood between us, looking from me to Rusty. "Whoa, whoa, whoa." He put his hands out and turned to me, confusion and worry all over his face. "That really true?" he asked, tentative, like he didn't really want to know. "About your brother?"

I bit my bottom lip and looked down at the ground, not wanting to answer. Because no matter how many times I'd said it to people in the last two weeks, people I knew, I hadn't really believed it. Even yesterday, at the funeral, I'd felt almost like an actor in a movie or something. But standing here, with Rusty throwing it in my face in front of a stranger sent a pain through me that was impossible to ignore. This was beyond forgivable.

A long moment passed without any of us speaking. A log popped, sending a tiny explosion of embers into the air. I leveled my eyes at Rusty and hoped he could feel how much I hated him right then. "It's true. My brother's dead."

"I'm sorry," Wyatt said softly. He reached for my hand, but I moved it away.

Rusty snorted. "Well, now. Looks like I ruined the mood."

He straightened up and looked over at Wyatt. "I'm sorry, man. She's all yours." Then he held out my own car keys to me. "Here you go, H. I'm guessin' I'll be sleeping under the stars tonight."

I smacked them out of his hand, into the dirt. "Screw you, Rusty."

He nodded like he deserved it, turned his back, and walked into the darkness, toward the road.

Wyatt waited until we couldn't see him anymore, then he picked up my keys, handed them to me gingerly. "Uh . . . you wanna stay a little while longer?"

I shook my head, on the verge of tears again.

"How 'bout I walk you back over to your car, then?"

I swallowed hard and nodded. "Okay."

We didn't say anything as we ducked through the bushes, and when we stood next to the car I could tell he was searching, maybe for the right thing to say. But there wasn't any right thing.

I shifted the keys in my hands. "Thanks for walking me."

His face was warm but serious. "Of course." He paused. "I know it's not my business, but don't let him make you feel bad. Everyone deals with stuff their own way, you know? I mean, that was a real shithead way to act, but you can tell he's broken up about it too." He smiled gently. "Anyway, I don't think there's anything wrong with you being here."

Wyatt, who I'd met hours earlier, peeing in my campsite, had somehow said the exact right thing. The kind of thing Finn would have said right before he would have convinced me to do something fun to get my mind off it. "Thank you." I sniffed. "I'm sorry about Rusty, he—"

Wyatt waved it off. "Don't worry about it. Come diving with us tomorrow. It'll feel good to see the sunrise. Like a fresh start." He gestured at the car. "I'll knock on the window."

I curled my fingers under the handle and took a deep breath. "All right." I meant to tell him thank you, but instead I dropped my hand, stood on tiptoe, and kissed his cheek.

He smiled, then took a step back. "Good night, Honor." Then he tipped his head, a small good night gesture that left me smiling myself.

Inside the car, I crawled in the backseat, spread my sleeping bag over it, and lay down so I could still see the stars out the window. I thought of Rusty somewhere out in the dark, and I wanted to hate him for what he'd said. But part of me wondered if he was right—if it was wrong of me to be here on this trip, if going to the concert was just a way of running away. What in the world would I tell Kyra Kelley about my brother, anyway? And why would she care?

I didn't have the energy or the heart to answer any of it. Every bit of me felt weighted down and tired. In the end, I settled for locking the doors, ensuring Rusty would have a lonely, uncomfortable night. Where, I didn't really care. Then I lay back and found Cygnus in the sky, watched his stars blink friendship and loss, honor and sacrifice, until all of it drifted off over the vastness of the desert.

7

A muted, repetitive *thunk* pulled at me from the other side of sleep. When I didn't move, it persisted. I made an honest effort to lift my eyelids, but it felt like I had only just closed them, and my mind fumbled for every possible reason to keep them that way: still dark, summertime, no school, nowhere I needed to be, no one who should be waking me up. . . .

I rolled over, expecting to snuggle down into my covers, but consciousness came down on me hard when my face found the cool vinyl of the backseat. I was in the car. Finn's car. At a campground in New Mexico, where Rusty had been awful and had walked off into the night and a boy I'd just met tried to make it better. But it wasn't better. Finn was still gone and I was still alone, and the heaviness of those things made me want to seal my eyes closed with the ridiculous hope that if I went back to sleep, none of it would be true.

The knocking stopped, but a loud whisper replaced it. "Honor! You awake?" *Thunk, thunk.* "If you still wanna dive, we're going." It was Wyatt's voice outside the window. Wyatt, who had been sweet and kind, and who I'd kissed on the cheek when he walked me to the car.

I let the last wisp of sleep slip away, then gave in and pushed myself up on the seat. I could see Wyatt's smile in the window before he took a step back so I could open the door. I looked in the rearview mirror, which wasn't much help in the dark, ran my fingers through my hair one quick time, pulled on my boots, and tried to put away the unsettled feeling that lingered from the night before. When I opened the door and breathed in the fresh smell of the dirt mingled with the crispness of the junipers and sage, it lifted ever so slightly.

"Mornin'." Wyatt stepped toward me and smiled. "You're a hard sleeper. Either that or you were just hoping I'd go away if you ignored me for long enough." He raised an eyebrow, then shoved his hands in his pockets and shivered a little. "You still wanna dive? Sam and Corrie are already over there getting the gear ready."

I hugged my arms to my chest and glanced around. "What time is it?"

"Five something. Sunrise is soon."

"I don't know. I . . ." I'd felt so much braver the night before, sitting next to the fire and planning an adventure, until Rusty'd gone and ruined it.

Wyatt motioned with his head at the picnic table. "He's out cold over there. I don't think he'll be up for a few hours."

I shook my head. "That's not what I meant. It's just . . . I don't know how to scuba dive, or what I'm supposed to do, or what I'm even doing here . . . and I should probably just get back on the road, because this whole thing is just—I'm kind of on a deadline. . . ." Wyatt nodded slowly as I stuttered, waiting for me to finish. A lump rose in my throat. "It sounded like a better idea in my head."

He shrugged simply. "That's okay. A lot of things do. You can just come watch if you want. There's a big rock you could sit on and see us from. And the sunrise'll still be great." He nodded over at where Rusty must've been laid out. "C'mon. He's not going anywhere."

I leaned against the car and considered again what it'd be like to see the stars from beneath the water and watch the sunlight wash over them, wiping the sky clean for a brand-new day. I needed one. Finn never would have passed up the chance. And he maybe even would have understood what I was doing here. I took a deep breath and looked up at the stars twinkling in the purple-black sky, then back to Wyatt. "Okay. I'll try it. Since I'm up and all."

Wyatt broke into a grin. "Got a bathing suit?"

I went to the trunk for it, and Wyatt followed. "I knew you had it in ya." He heaved a large bag over one shoulder, then looped his other arm through mine. "Let's move on out."

It didn't look like the sun had any plans to come up soon, but according to Wyatt it would, so we needed to hurry. We jogged across the deserted highway, and he ducked under a chain that was stretched across the entrance to the parking lot for the dive center, holding it up for me to do the same.

"Are we sneaking in here?"

He glanced back at me. "Sort of. It's just not open yet, is

all." He stopped and hitched his bag back up on his shoulder for the tenth time since we'd left the campsite. "I don't think anyone will be out here for a while, though. Only Corrie would come up with something like this. She's . . . creative."

I smiled. "Do you guys do this a lot? Come up with random adventures that you go on together?"

"They try to make a thing of it, Sam and Corrie. They're good together that way. They're all into that whole carpe diem thing." He was a little out of breath from lugging his bag. "And usually, they don't mind if I come, which is cool. Sam's pretty mellow as far as older brothers go."

He stopped short, like he'd said something wrong, and neither one of us said anything as our feet crunched over the gravel in the empty parking lot. We came to a low rock wall, where Wyatt set his bag down. He looked at me, concerned. "I'm sorry. I didn't mean to—"

This time it was me who stopped him. "It's okay. You can say the word 'brother.' It's fine." I looked past the wall and caught a glimpse of the water's slick, black surface. "His name was Finn." I paused at the pang in my chest and waited for it to pass. "Anyway, he would have thought this was great."

Wyatt nodded but was quiet.

"And I think he would have liked you, too. Rusty was just being a jerk last night for whatever reason."

"Whatever reason, huh?" He raised his eyebrows. "Yeah . . . I don't know what *that* reason could be." He held my eyes a moment, and I decided not to bother explaining that it wasn't a protective thing or a jealous thing. It was an asshole thing. Wyatt clapped his hands together. "You ready? It's right over there."

We climbed over the wall and made our way down the slope to where Sam and Corrie's silhouettes whispered as they cinched straps and clicked together buckles. Corrie saw us first and came over to me, arms wide. "You made it!" She gave me an awkward, equipment-laden hug, then pulled me back by my shoulders. "You nervous? Don't be. Here." She grabbed my hand and led me over to a bench carved into the surrounding rocks. "Wyatt can get you all set up. We need to hurry if we wanna beat the sunrise."

I looked back at Wyatt and thought for a second I should tell him that Rusty never needed any reason to act the way he did. You never knew what you might get with him. But he had already taken his bag over to where Sam was, and they were laughing together as he unzipped it and began pulling out equipment. I looked around. Even in the dark I could tell the Blue Hole was big. Bigger than any swimming pool I'd been in. I pulled off my boots and let my toes press into the cool stone that lined the edge.

"So, this is natural? Nobody put it here?"

"Nope." Corrie stepped next to me. "All natural. Crazy that it's here in the middle of the desert, huh? Wait till you see it in the light. It's the most perfect shade of blue you've ever seen." She handed me a thin shirt. "Here. Put this on over your bathing suit. It's a rash guard. The water's pretty warm, but this'll help a little bit to keep your heat."

I set it down and glanced around for a place to change.

"Don't worry, it's dark. They won't see you from over there."

"True." I nodded and stepped back into the wall—as much as I could, anyway, while Corrie put on what looked like a backpack with the scuba tank attached to it. "I'll see you over there," she said. "You're going to love this."

A wave of nervousness went through me. "Okay."

In the dark, I changed into my bathing suit beneath my dress without too much trouble. Once it was tied, I pulled the dress over my head and replaced it with Corrie's rash guard, which fit smooth and tight.

"Hey." Wyatt came back over, wearing just his trunks. "Here," he said. "I'm gonna give you just a little bit of weight to help you sink when we get in."

"Sink?" That just sounded bad. I preferred to swim, or float, like Lilah and I and whatever boys she rounded up did on the river on hot summer days. "I don't know . . ."

"You'll be fine," Wyatt said, holding up a belt with two pouches on it. "Put your arms up." I did, and he slid the belt around my waist. I kept my eyes down, trying not to smile as his hands brushed my stomach and cinched it tight. "That feel all right?"

He was looking at me, close, and smiling just as cute as he had the night before.

"Yeah." I dropped my eyes back to the belt that hung heavy on my hips and forced back the fluttery smile that crept over me. "That's, um . . . that's good." He stepped back, and I rolled my eyes in the dark at the sudden nervousness that tingled in my stomach.

Sam came over, already wearing his air tank on his back. "We don't have any extra fins, but you'll be hooked up with Wyatt anyhow." There was a smile in his voice as he said it, and my cheeks burned despite the cool morning air. He turned to Wyatt. "You guys can just follow the line down.

That way, you'll know how deep you are. Don't take her any deeper than twenty or so, okay?"

Wyatt nodded.

"Corrie and I need to get in so we can make it to the bottom in time for the sunrise." He turned back to me, his voice reassuring. "Wyatt'll take you through what to do, but really, you just have to breathe nice and slow, and stay relaxed. He'll do the rest."

Wyatt nudged me with his shoulder. "Remember, good hands."

I looked at the black water and took a deep breath. "I don't know why, but I trust you."

Sam gave my shoulder a squeeze, then walked over to a ramp at the edge of the hole, where Corrie was waiting. She stood on her tiptoes and kissed him before their silhouettes disappeared with a splash into the water. A light flicked on below the surface and illuminated them in the center of a cloud of bubbles, ringed by a blue-green circle of light.

As they started to sink, the light grew dimmer, creating a deep green glow in the middle of the large pool. Aside from the soft gurgle of air bubbles breaking the water's surface, the morning was perfectly still, and in that moment it seemed so beautifully fragile that neither one of us spoke. There, in the quiet space between the stars above us and the fading light below, everything in me seemed to soften just a little.

We stayed there like that, so quiet, until Wyatt spoke—reluctant, I imagined, to break the silence. "Worth it to wake up at dark thirty, right?" He was watching the same circle of light as it faded.

I stared at it, trying to etch the image in my mind before

turning to him. "Yeah. This is beautiful. Thank you for getting me."

He held my eyes for a long moment. "Wait till you see it from under the water." He pointed to the pool, now only faintly lit. "Come on. I'll show you what to do."

It was a strange sensation, continuing to take in a breath, even as I dipped below the surface of the water. I concentrated on breathing slow and steady like Sam and Wyatt had both said, and the sound of the air moving through the hose made it easy to stay focused on that. My legs brushed against Wyatt's in the dark of the water, and I was conscious of how close we were at that moment, literally breathing the same air. It sent a little zing through me, and I shivered despite the surprising warmth of the water. He clicked on his small dive light and pointed to his ears, indicating for me to pop mine. Then he smiled beneath his mask and flashed the okay sign. When I answered with my own, he grabbed the rope I already had a hold on, and then pointed down, to where it disappeared into darkness.

I took another exaggerated breath, and we began to walk our hands down the rope, alternating one after another, down through the water. Our bubbles danced around each other, then sailed upward, leaving a sparkling trail back to the surface. I hadn't expected the water to be so still or clear, but it was, and our tiny light bounced off the limestone walls of the hole, throwing wavy shadows all around us. I didn't feel the pull of the weight belt, didn't notice the pressure I had been nervous about. I was floating downward without the sensation of falling. Sinking, even though I felt weightless.

We went slowly, face to face, Wyatt constantly checking to see if I was all right, me assuring us both that I was. The deepest I'd ever been underwater was the bottom of Lilah's pool. We'd spent every summer afternoon there for as long as I could remember, all the way back from the days of 'Marco Polo' and 'Sharks and Minnows' to this summer, which we mostly spent soaking up both the sun and the last of our time together before we left for different schools. We'd lie there with our magazines and our straps hanging untied until we couldn't stand the heat anymore and had to get in. Lilah didn't get her hair wet anymore, just in case she needed to look cute for one of her many admirers who might drop by. By the time we were juniors, she could have her pick.

I dove in, though, sure that my hair didn't really matter. I'd yet to have a boy become a boyfriend. As soon as it looked like it might happen, Finn and Rusty were right there to scare the crap out of him, and I was unceremoniously blown off. So, while Lilah got sunscreen rubbed onto her back, I swam. My favorite moment was always the one when I reached the bumpy bottom of the pool, where the only sound was the crackling of the turquoise water all around me. It was well worth the tangly hair and smudged mascara.

As we descended, I wondered if I could have talked Lilah into scuba diving in the dark with a stranger, in a mask that even made cute, cute Wyatt look silly. I watched our hands leapfrog each other down the rope, brushing each time they did, and figured probably not.

When Wyatt's hand landed on a black line, he motioned for me to stop, and I realized we must've hit twenty feet. He pointed to his ears again, and I pinched my nose and blew gently, relieving a bit of pressure. I gave him the okay sign, and he pointed to his light, then up to the surface, asking me with his eyes if I was ready for him to turn it off. I took in one more slow breath, let it out, and nodded, just as it went dark.

For half a second, I panicked.

But then Wyatt's hands found mine on the rope, and he held them firmly enough that I relaxed. He waited a moment, then let go. Water swirled by as he swam behind me and grabbed the rope again, so that his arms were wrapped securely around me, anchored by his hands on mine. I wondered if he could hear the unevenness of my breaths at that moment. Our legs tangled languidly there in the dark, and we stayed like that, suspended vertically together, for a long moment before he peeled my fingers, one by one, off the rope. I let him, and when the last one was free, his hands went to my waist and gently pulled me back with him until I was lying back with my eyes to the surface. They caught a tiny light, waving down through the water, and then another and another. Stars twinkled in the paling sky, sending light from the past all the way down to us.

Suspended as we were, with no horizon line or landscape or anything else to draw a separation between the water and sky, I pictured us up there with the stars. Another story written in tiny lights. We were a constellation put in the sky—two people holding hands, floating peacefully above everything else, in a beautiful, perfect moment.

Finn told me once, as we sat on the porch watching the sun go down, that one thing he remembered our mom telling him was that life sometimes gives you a tiny moment of peace when you need it most. And that you had to be careful and look out for it or you'd miss it. He'd said it just as the last sliver of sun dipped below the horizon, leaving a flaming pink summer sky behind. We sat quiet in the still heat, and I'd thought I understood what he meant then, because it felt so good and safe to be sitting there with him next to me. Now though, I understood it with a depth that made me want to laugh and cry at the same time, and I wished more than anything I could tell him.

Wyatt squeezed my hand, and it was light enough now that I could see his free hand pointing to a tree silhouetted against the pale morning sky, one tiny star barely visible above it. I blinked and it was gone. The others dissolved into the morning almost as quickly and were replaced by a cloudless swath of pale sky, tinged blue around the edges. Above the surface, it might have been a moment where I glanced over at Wyatt and he understood. He would've maybe even leaned in and kissed it softly into my memory. It might have made me feel less lonely and lost. But beneath the water, we didn't move and we didn't speak, and my moment of peace faded slowly into the blue around us.

8

"That was amazing! Wasn't that amazing?!" Corrie lifted her mask, clearly euphoric as we bobbed on the surface.

"Best idea you've ever had," Sam agreed, sending a spray of water droplets high in the air.

"Hands down, best moment of this trip. Aside from meeting my dream girl, of course." Wyatt looked over at me, and his gentle brown eyes searched mine for some sort of reaction. There really had been a moment there with him, beneath the blue of the water, but it wasn't the kind of moment he meant. I didn't say anything, but managed a feeble smile and a nod, and when I felt the lump rise at the back of my throat, I knew I couldn't trust my voice.

Wyatt's eyebrows drew together, and he dipped his chin into the water, blew a few bubbles. Sam and Corrie looked from me to each other, and I knew I was acting odd. I knew

I should have been giddy and laughing like they were when they surfaced. I should have been elated and proud that I'd tried something so out of my small range of experience. I should have smiled or squeezed Wyatt's hand, which still held my own. But all at once, I wanted to get out and go far away from the possibility of losing it in front of them all. I didn't want to cry over Finn in front of them—in front of anyone, for that matter.

For a long time after our parents died, I cried a lot. Anything set me off, and nothing anyone said or did made it any better—except for Finn. He knew what to say, or what not to say. And he never cried. Not that I ever saw, at least. He was the strong one of the two of us, and if I gave in and let myself cry for him now, there'd be nobody there to stop it.

I let go of Wyatt's hand and looked over at the ramp we'd used to get in. He nodded wordlessly, and we made our way to the edge together, leaving Sam and Corrie floating in the middle of the blue. When my toes scraped the rough stone of the bottom, I stood slowly, avoiding Wyatt's eyes, and began to unhook myself. My fingers fumbled when they got to the buckle of the weight belt around my waist, and I clamped my lips together, angry at this little thing that was about to break me.

"Here." Wyatt's hand stilled my own. "I'll get that one. It jams sometimes." I let my arms fall at my sides, and he unclicked it easily, then bent down and forced me to meet his eyes. Water droplets still clung to his face. "You seem like you're not okay."

I bit the inside of my cheek and looked down. "I'm sorry. That really was beautiful, and you . . . it's just . . ."

"It's all right." He bumped my shoulder gently with his.

"I have that speechless effect on a lot of girls, really." I smiled but didn't say anything. When he spoke next, it was softened, sincere. "I'm really sorry about your brother, Honor. I'd be a lost wreck if something like that happened to Sam. But you seem strong to me, which means you're probably doing things right. Like I said, people deal with stuff in all different ways, and maybe you're someone who needs to keep moving. . . ." He kind of trailed off, maybe realizing what that meant.

My eyes went to his, and I felt a rush of gratitude for Wyatt. For the second time, he had said the right thing at the exact moment I needed it. I didn't know how he could understand, but that didn't really matter.

"Thank you" was what I said, but there was so much more behind it, it didn't seem enough. I wanted to tell him that he was the kind of person you don't meet very often—one who is good and kind and really *sees* people. The kind I wished I'd met under different circumstances, when I wasn't in the middle of a ridiculous road trip, with Rusty tagging along, and an impossible goal. The kind of guy I might have fallen for without a second thought.

Instead, I stood on my tiptoes, wrapped my arms around his neck, and whispered it again. "Thank you, Wyatt, for saying that, and thank you for . . . this." I gestured at the water behind him. "It was perfect." His arms came around my waist and, despite the coolness of his skin, wrapped me in solid warmth. Where the general's arms around me had communicated a respect and shared grief, Wyatt's were comfort and compassion. And I wanted to stay like that as long as I could, because I knew that on the other side, I'd keep moving, like he had said.

I was pretty sure he knew too, because when we let go of each other, he stood there looking at me the way you look at something you wish you could have but know you really can't. He smiled at me, sad, in the warm morning light, and we were one of those songs that talk about a missed moment or chance that you go back and think about over and over, wondering, *What if?*

He straightened his shoulders and shook the disappointment from his smile. "Well . . . we should maybe get back . . . before your good ol' boy wakes up and thinks you ran off with me or something." He held my eyes a long moment. Long enough to be an invitation.

"Wouldn't want him to think that." I sighed, wishing for a second I could accept. And then I just stood there. I didn't want to move from where we were or go back to Rusty or leave here with one of those "what if" moments to wonder about down the road—literally. Instead, I took a step into Wyatt, stood once again on my tiptoes, and kissed him lightly on surprised lips that took a heartbeat to catch up. It didn't last more than a few seconds, but when we pulled back and smiled shyly at each other, it felt a little more like a sweet conclusion than a missed chance.

That sweetness lasted even after we exchanged phone numbers, promises to keep in touch, and more than one lingering hug. It lasted right up until I ducked through the trail in the bushes between our campsites. And then it ended abruptly. Just as I saw Rusty leaning shirtless into the open hood of the Impala. He stood casually at the sound of my footsteps, and I felt myself tense up with irritation as he wiped the grease from his hands on his balled-up shirt. He eyed me a moment, then shut the hood, hard.

"Mornin'."

He said it just like nothing. Just like he hadn't been a total ass the night before, just like he figured I'd forgiven him and all was well. He didn't even ask how the dive was or if I was okay. Which made me even more angry. I'd expected him to be asleep still when I got back, or maybe awake and wondering when I'd be back, feeling bad for what he'd said the night before. Instead, he was up, showered, and indifferent. I walked past him without saying anything and leaned into the driver's side to pop the trunk.

"When's the last time you got this thing a tune-up?" He leaned against the hood, squinting into the sun.

I ignored him and huffed back to the trunk, pulled out underwear, a tank top, and a pair of cutoffs. And socks, too, for under my boots. I didn't want to give him anything to complain about. Then I ducked behind the open trunk and rearranged my towel so I could change beneath it.

Rusty raised his voice over the trunk. "Looks like it's been awhile. You're lucky nothing's gone wrong." His words left off, and I heard the unmistakable crunch of boots over dirt as he came back to where I was changing. "You listenin'?" I yanked my top over my head and pulled it down, lightning quick, before I dropped the towel.

"Oh." He stopped short as I smoothed my shorts over my legs.

I rolled my eyes, then leveled them right at him. "I heard you, Rusty. And yeah, it's probably been a while, but it's not the car that something's gone wrong with, it's you." My voice came out icy. "Actually, it's *all* wrong, if you haven't noticed. See . . . my brother's dead. Oh, wait—you reminded me of that last night in front of everyone." Something like confusion, or shock, spread over his face, and I stepped right up into it, strengthened by his reaction. I lowered my voice. "But. My brother, who used to be your best friend, sent me this letter and these tickets, and now I'm on this trip, which wouldn't be so bad, except for . . . *you*." He flinched, and I took a step back, losing a little of my bluster. I looked at the ground and hoped he couldn't see that I'd gone from shaking mad to hurt left over from the night before. And now my voice faltered more than a little. "You had no right last night."

He didn't say anything.

"And you have no right to say *anything* about how I handle this. *You* let him go, a long time ago." It was cruel, I knew, because no matter how it had been between them when Finn left, I knew how much Rusty cared about him before, and that wasn't the kind of thing that just disappeared all of a sudden. But once Finn enlisted, Rusty wrote him off, and that was a complete mystery to me. Best friends don't do that. And if he was gonna tell me how wrong it was to be here the day after we buried him, I was gonna let him know how much more wrong it was to turn your back on a person who mattered to you.

Rusty was silent. Jaw-clenched silent.

And then I was too, and we stood there fuming at each other in the middle of the desert in New Mexico, with the heat beginning to rise all around and who knows how many miles in front of us.

He gave first. Looked at the ground, cleared his throat, and nodded. Then he raised his chin and stared right at me, and I saw something I thought I recognized in the green of his eyes. Sincerity, maybe.

"I'm sorry, H. About what I said last night." He paused. "I didn't have any right." I waited. First, because it sounded genuine, and second, because I wasn't ready to forgive him yet. He looked at the car, shiny black in the morning sun, and when his eyes came back to me, it seemed like a tiny thing had shifted somehow. For a moment, anyway. Then he held his hands out to his sides in a question. "What do you want me to do? To make it up?"

That was it? I fought the urge to shake him and realized that this might actually be the best he could do. And I was worn out. And starving.

"Buy breakfast," I said flatly. A slow, knowing smile crept over his stubbly face, and I rolled my eyes. But I dug in my bag anyway and came up with Finn's beat-up leather key chain looped around my finger. "And then drive awhile."

I glanced out the window as I pulled out of our spot, and a twinge of emptiness hit me as we rolled past Wyatt's bare campsite and back onto the road. It was that same emptiness that's there when you wake up in the middle of one of those perfect dreams you can't get back to, no matter how hard you try. I thought of his phone number tucked away in my purse and knew I would probably never call, because that's just what Wyatt had been. A good dream that would linger a while and eventually melt into a tiny wisp of a feeling.

9

We didn't say much over breakfast. I asked him to pass the syrup. He asked the waitress for more coffee. The clinking-dishes-and-fork restaurant noise and chatter of summer travelers ready to hit the road filled in the background until we finished. But when we stepped out the door and headed to the Pala, there was no avoiding it. I was still tense. I'd let go of being mad at him, but I wasn't sure how to go back to acting normal around him. Whatever that meant now. For his part, Rusty didn't seem to notice. The parking lot was already baking, sending wobbly waves of heat up to the cloudless sky, and I tried to think of ways to avoid strained silence in the car—small talk, loud music, windows rolled down, feigned sleep . . . With him there, this was gonna be a much longer trip than if I'd taken it alone.

Rusty stopped at the hood. "You still want me to drive?"

I nodded and tossed the keys over to him. "Yeah." I almost said something about how long it had probably been since he'd driven or even ridden in the Pala before yesterday, but I stopped short, realizing that could be a tangly path to go down.

He swung open the heavy door and ducked into the car, and I did the same. We yanked them shut, almost at the same time, then sat there a moment in the obvious quiet that followed. I searched for something to say to fill it up, because the thing that was between us now wasn't him being a jerk or me being mad. It was that small space in the car, with just him and me and no Finn. We both felt it.

Rusty looked like he was about to say something, then put the key in and revved the engine instead. He turned up the radio, adjusted the mirrors, got reacquainted, then sat back and surveyed the view from behind the wheel. "It's been a while, Pala." He gave the dash a satisfied pat and grinned over at me, one eyebrow raised. "California? Go see what's-her-name's concert?"

I wasn't sure if he was mocking me or if he really meant it. "Her name's Kyra Kelley. And you should stop acting like you don't know who she is, since you once rode in *this* car to one of *her* concerts, then drooled the whole time she was up on the stage. And yes, going to her show is still the plan, unless you can think of something better." I said it like I was still absolutely sure, then waited for the smart-ass comment that was sure to follow.

Rusty put his arm on the seat behind me and cranked the wheel hard as he backed out. "I can think of a helluva lot better things than that, but this is your deal and your car, so . . ." He twisted back around and put the car into drive. "You're the boss." With that, he laid hard into the gas, gunning us out of the parking lot and back out onto the dusty I-40 with a jump. It was kind of charming in his redneck, Rusty sort of way, and I forgot for a moment what the other side of that coin looked like.

Out the windshield, the road stretched forever in front of us, an endless strip of black dividing the cracked dirt of the desert. The sky expanded brilliant blue in every direction, and the sheer vastness of it made the morning feel full of possibility. I rolled my window down all the way and stuck an arm out into the heat, soaking it up. In about two blinks, we flew past a sign that read YOU ARE NOW LEAVING SANTA ROSA. COME AGAIN!, and as we did I heard the familiar first notes of "Wayward Son," one of Finn's favorite songs of all time. Also one that I used to put up a big fuss about, rolling my eyes and covering my ears. I'd thought it was the cheesiest song ever. He'd loved it for that. Rusty looked over at me with a cool smile, then nodded and cranked up the volume just in time for the chorus to open up:

"Carry on my wayward son,
there'll be peace when you are done."

I sat back in the seat and opened my mouth to protest, but he shook his head. "Nobody talks during 'Wayward Son.' Car rules." He turned the volume up another notch.

I tried to hide it, tried to look exasperated, but it was no use. I felt a true, happy smile rise in me as Rusty sang along. He pounded a fist on the wheel to the beat, and I rolled my eyes again, even though I was about to join in. I liked this.

This moment. It was one Finn would have loved, and I pictured us kicking up a billowing trail of dust as we headed out into the great wide open, in honor of him.

Easy silence settled between us as we sailed over mile after mile of flat, brown desert. It felt different in the passenger seat, with Rusty driving steady and fast. He seemed at home in Finn's car, like he belonged there as much as me. And to tell the honest truth, he did. It was Rusty who had gone with Finn to talk its previous owner into selling it to a fifteen-year-old without a license for half the asking price. Finn had worked all summer, hauling dirt and doing whatever else at a neighbor's ranch, and he'd decided this was the car.

It was a piece at the time, all peeling paint and torn vinyl, probably worth closer to what he had in his pocket than what the guy was asking. But when they rolled into Aunt Gina's driveway in it, he and Rusty were kings. Kings who spent every waking moment working on that car and emerged from the garage covered in grease and boy stink.

I mostly tried to steer clear when Rusty was out there. He was the type of boy who'd either come at me with the hose on full blast or completely ignore me while he and Finn talked about Sydney Bennett, the senior girl Finn (along with the entire male population at school) loved from afar. She was a girl of myth and legend who stopped even the most cocky guys in their tracks with her long dark hair, blue eyes, and smile that was just the right combination of naughty and nice. She had perfected the art of hinting at possibility—a smile or a fleeting moment of eye contact that could keep a guy hoping for god only knew how long.

I knew all this from listening behind the half-open door between the garage and the kitchen, and I would've given anything to learn just how she did it. They talked about her outfits and speculated about what type of underwear she'd been wearing, if any. They proudly rehashed any little moment she gave them, whether she'd passed them in the hallway and glanced in their direction or smiled at them from the top of the cheer pyramid. Never mind that Finn and Rusty each had their fair share of football groupies who were more than happy to throw themselves pathetically at their feet. They would've traded any of those girls in a second for Sydney Bennett. Being sophomores, they never had a shot in hell with her, but they worked on that car like it would somehow give them one.

Once Rusty went home, I'd head out to the garage and survey their progress. I had no idea how they knew how to work on the car and was half-amazed whenever they did it right. Finn always claimed that once a guy turned thirteen, he automatically knew everything. He told me that every time I asked him how he knew how to do something, and after a while, I mostly believed him. I even thought maybe once I turned thirteen I'd know all the girl things I needed to know, like how to do a smoky eye or walk like Sydney Bennett or look at a guy and say a whole lot without saying anything. But thirteen came and went, and I was none the wiser about any of it.

Lilah was a lot better than me at all those things, and she did her best to help me along, whether it was talking me into wearing something I had no idea I could pull off or starting up a conversation with the boys we had crushes on and somehow working me in so that I became a part of it. And I loved her for all those things, but back then I was most myself when I sat with my legs dangling out the Pala, while Finn worked and made plans for everything—the next football game, the upcoming summer, his senior year, college with Rusty, everything. I'd be willing to bet he spent his free moments on the other side of the world planning what he'd do when he got back.

Before I fell too deep into the sadness of the thought, Rusty turned the radio down. "She's runnin' a little warm," he said. He looked over at me when I didn't answer. "The car."

"What's that mean?" I hoped hard it was nothing. We didn't need car trouble in the middle of the nowhere. I couldn't afford it. I'd planned on sleeping in the car and eating cheap. There was no room in my budget for a motel, let alone for the car to break down. And Kyra Kelley wasn't going to postpone her last show for us.

Rusty chewed the toothpick he'd had in his teeth since we left the restaurant. "I dunno. Maybe just needs some more water." He shrugged. "Or it could be somethin' else."

I looked across the expanse of shrub-dotted desert. The dark outline of mountains stood barely visible in the distance. In between us and them was absolute nothingness, except for cracked dirt and a lone airplane streak across the cobalt sky. "So . . . what are we supposed to do, then?" I watched Rusty for some sort of clue and tried to keep from sounding panicky.

He flicked the toothpick up and down between his front teeth, thinking. "How bad you wanna go to that concert?"

He said it like it was a perfectly acceptable idea now, which

I appreciated. Because it still sounded ridiculous out loud. But then it didn't. I knew it would've been near impossible and obscenely expensive to get those tickets here in the States. Yet Finn somehow did it from his dusty base camp in the middle of a war. It felt like I owed it to him.

I tapped my toes on the floor. "Bad enough to wanna keep going." It came out sounding unsure, more like a question than an answer. Rusty didn't say anything, so I turned to him directly. "You think it'll be all right to make it there?" I thought of Finn's letter in my purse and his one simple request. "It has to be."

Rusty breathed in deep, like he was about to say something important. Then he shrugged like he couldn't care less. "Maybe. If not, we can stop off at my mom's. Work on it there."

I opened my mouth to say something, but habit kept me quiet. Since Rusty was fourteen and she took off, his mom was a topic I'd always figured it was best not to mention, but now he brought her up like it was nothing at all. He must've seen my reaction, because his eyes flicked over to me a second, then back to the road. He shifted the toothpick in his mouth.

"She lives in Sedona. Came to my games once I was at school. I went down to her house a time or two." I nodded, knowing better than to ask any more than he was willing to tell, but curious all the same. He never talked about her after she left. I hadn't known where she was or if they spoke or anything. I wondered if, when he'd gotten to school up there, he'd been the one to get in touch with her or if it was the other way around. Maybe he'd gotten homesick for someone who knew him, or maybe she felt guilty and wanted to know her son again. He didn't leave any room for questions, though. His eyes slid over to me again, and he laughed a little. "She won't even *recognize* you."

I didn't know if it was his tone or his face, but something caught me in the way he said it, and a little nervous tingle went through me. I straightened up and looked out the window, conscious all of a sudden of his eyes on me. Then I caught a flyaway strand of hair and twisted it around my fingers. "Why?" I asked, a little too loudly.

Rusty smirked and put his eyes back on the road. "Nothin', H."

Irritated, I reached down for a package of licorice I'd stashed in my bag. "You shouldn't do that, you know."

"Do what?"

"*That.* Where you say something like it's some sort of joke or like it means something and then just say, 'Nothing, H.'" I imitated his nonchalant answer in the worst possible way, mocking myself, really.

Rusty raised his eyebrows and smirked again, not bothering to hide that this was all very entertaining for him. He reached over and grabbed the piece of licorice I'd just pulled from the package, right out of my hand, and took a bite. Then he talked and chewed at the same time. "You just . . . grew up is all."

I pulled another twist out of the package, bit into it, and rolled my eyes even though I was flattered just a tiny bit. "Well. Nice of you to notice."

"I didn't. Not until Willy or Walter or whatever his name was got all stupid over you and your smelly-ass boots." He laughed.

Oh. I pressed my lips together and nodded, my little bubble of pride burst by the realization of what he was getting at. What else did I expect?

"*Wyatt.* His name was Wyatt." I tried to think of something to say in his defense, but I knew whatever I came up with wouldn't make a difference. Rusty would just make a joke out of him, so I let it go and squinted at the rolling backs of the hills on the horizon. Wyatt was sweet and sincere and had given me a few moments of understanding and kindness. Rusty didn't need to go on and ruin it.

Out the corner of my eye, I watched him nod slowly, and I knew he wasn't finished. "Wyatt. That's right." I didn't say anything, and Rusty spit the toothpick out his open window before turning back to me. "Y'all go swimmin' this morning?" His tone had shifted the tiniest bit—less sarcasm, more curiosity.

I was still wary of the conversation, but it gave me some small satisfaction to tell him. "Scuba diving. We watched the sun come up from under the water." I paused, surprised that along with the image in my mind came the same sadness that was there before. "It was the prettiest thing I've ever seen." My voice wavered a little. Rusty didn't say anything, but I saw him look at me in the mirror. I bit the inside of my cheek and turned toward the window, letting the hot wind rush over my face.

After a long moment, he did something that surprised me. A small thing that just about did me in, coming from him. He wrapped a warm hand around the back of my neck and squeezed gently. And for the first time since we'd left, he said something right.

"Finn woulda loved that, you know. That you did that." He paused a beat, looked right at me quick, then away again. "He'd be proud of you, H."

The yellow line I'd been watching out my window blurred, and I swallowed red licorice over the lump in my throat. Rusty squeezed my neck again, and when he pulled his hand away I wished for a sliver of a moment he would have left it, warm and sure on my bare shoulder.

I looked at him then and said the only thing I could. "I miss him." Rusty's jaw tightened, and he shifted in the seat. "I miss him so much."

He glanced at the side mirror, then back to the road. "Me too, H. I miss him too."

We didn't say anything else for a long time. Just kinda let it hang there that we were actually together on something. After a while, my eyes got heavy and I leaned my head on the seat. Sleep was closing in fast, the kind you know is going to take you under deep, and I was running out of fight.

In between long blinks, I watched Rusty sit back in the seat, one easy hand on the wheel, and more than once thought I felt his eyes on me. But I could've been dreaming by then. Either way, at that moment, in the rumbling cab of the Pala, he felt like the only other person in the world who might be feeling the very same thing as me. And that in itself was a comfort.

10

I had to pee in the worst, gut-clenching, leg-crossing kind of way, and no amount of distraction was gonna help. I glanced over at Rusty, trying to gauge if he'd drunk his whole soda and might need to stop soon. I didn't want to be the one to make us stop twice in a row. I'd already made him pull into a dusty little gas station when I woke up over an hour ago, and the stop that was supposed to be a quick run-in-and-out ended up taking over fifteen minutes while the crackly old guy behind the counter schooled me on the dangers of driving the highway in the middle of monsoon season. I assured him I wasn't alone and even bought an extra jug of water along with my other road snacks because he insisted it was important to have. Which made me laugh, since it seemed to me the last thing you'd need more of in a monsoon was water.

When I got back, Rusty took one look at the gallon of

water and giant sodas and shook his head. "You drink all that, we'll be stopping every damn hour for you to pee."

"I'm not gonna drink it all. One's for you. Here." I handed him a Coke and set the water jug in the backseat. "The water's in case we get caught in a monsoon."

He just looked at me like I'd said something stupid as I ducked in out of the swirling wind and yanked the door shut.

"Long story. Never mind." I clicked the seat belt across my lap and reached for the wrinkled map on the floor. "How far do you think we can make it today if we go without stopping?"

Rusty put the car in gear and shrugged. "If I keep driving and you don't need to stop eight more times?" He took a long gulp of his soda and pulled back out onto the empty highway. "We could go forever."

"Could we?" I looked up from the map momentarily, then felt a little ridiculous. I hadn't meant it to sound so . . . like every other girl who talked to him.

Rusty didn't answer. Just put his eyes on the road and let the hint of a smirk cross his face, which brought me right back to irritated. I turned up the radio, grabbed my Kyra Kelley magazine from the gas station the day before, and did my best to look occupied while resolving not to make a fool of myself in front of him for the rest of the trip. And to make sure that the next time we stopped, it wasn't because of me.

That was almost two hours ago, and now I was gonna burst. I'd spent the time eating and drinking and fiddling with whatever I could to pass the time and make it not so awkward while Rusty drove along silently. We'd given up on music after a while, since there was nothing but static on the radio and I wasn't about to plug in my iPod again. Every so often, Rusty would run a careless hand through his hair or stretch his legs out a bit, but that was it. He seemed like he was off in his own thoughts, so I let him be.

I glanced out the window, hoping for a sign saying it was only a few miles to another little podunk town, or a rest stop—even a bush would have sufficed at this point. But there was only flat, brown desert and a horizon rimmed with clouds. And wind. I could see it sweeping over the ground, kicking up miniature dust devils off in the distance. It made me think of clips on the news or bits in the newspaper that told all about how harsh the weather was over in the deserts where our troops were deployed. How sandstorms would tear through, blasting everything in their paths, making it difficult to see or even breathe. I'd asked Finn about it once in an e-mail, and he downplayed it, saying it wasn't that bad, and whenever it happened they just had to hunker down and wait it out. I looked over at Rusty, who seemed tired, and the thought occurred to me that maybe that's what we were doing together in the cab of the Pala, on the dusty highway. Riding out the storm Finn's absence left behind. Maybe that's why Rusty was so quiet. I glanced at him again out the corner of my eye, and he must've felt it, because his eyes flicked over in my direction.

"Hand me that cup down there."

"It's empty."

"I know that. I gotta take a piss." He motioned with his head at the Coke cup by my feet.

"Are you *kidding* me?"

"I look like I'm kidding you?" He unbuckled his belt. "Just gimme the cup and look the other way. I gotta go."

"No." Not only did the thought of him peeing into my empty soda cup right next to me repulse me, but bending in half to reach it when I had to go as bad as I did would surely put me over the edge. And I was desperate enough now to crouch behind the car myself. "Why don't you just pull over? Like a normal person?"

Rusty cracked a sunflower seed between his teeth and spit the shell out the window. "Fine." He looked in the rearview mirror briefly before pulling onto the dirt shoulder. "Then you're driving awhile. I'm beat."

We each took a turn with our business out in the hot wind, which wasn't an easy task. For me at least. When I got back in, Rusty was stretched out across the backseat, hands behind his head, grinning up at the ceiling.

"Get any on your boots?"

"Oh my god, shut up."

He propped his heels up on the back armrest. "What? I did. It's windy out there."

I turned the key and revved the engine, adjusting the mirrors back down to my eye level. "Charming. And I thought girls liked you for your jock status, not your conversational skills."

"There's a lot they like about me, H, but it doesn't have much to do with football. Or conversation." I couldn't see his face in the mirror, but I could hear the smug smile in his voice.

"Okay, you can stop now. I don't need to know anymore."

"Just sayin' . . ."

A gust of wind blasted the windshield with sand as I pulled us back onto the highway and gave it some gas.

"Might wanna close those vents. Wind's picking up out there. And slow down if that sand kicks up. Can't see ten feet in front of you when it really gets going. And—"

"You wanna drive?"

"Sure don't."

"Then leave me alone about it. I've been driving this thing ever since Finn left."

A steady wind sprayed the windshield with dust, like rain, and Rusty's boots tapped against the window, but there was no answer from the backseat. I brought my eyes back to the road and the sky, which had gotten three shades darker in the space of a minute.

I snapped the vents shut. "You know what I will never understand?"

"What's that?"

"Why he went in the first place." When Finn first told me about his decision to enlist, I thought it was a joke. When his face went serious and his tone resolute, I realized it wasn't, but I wasn't about to let it go. I'd pleaded with him over and over to explain it to me. To justify it. And some small part of me was convinced that all my questioning and doubt would somehow be enough to change his mind. But every time, his simple answer, which simultaneously frustrated and terrified me, was that it was the right thing to do. And I'd wanted to argue a million different reasons why it wasn't and why he shouldn't, but the only one I could come up with was me. I never said it, though, because if I did and he still went, what did that mean?

That I wasn't enough reason to stay? That he didn't need me as much as I needed him? That he was tired of me needing him?

"You and me both." Rusty let out a sigh, and I watched in the mirror as he sat up, no trace left of his smile. "We never did see eye to eye on that. Me and him." He looked out the back window, kept his eyes away from the mirror. "That's why things got rough with us, I guess."

I watched him in the mirror a long moment, waiting for him to explain, but he didn't, and it made me wonder if maybe Rusty had asked Finn why he was going, argued with him over it, and come away not liking the answer. The only other person who needed Finn as much as I did was him. They'd called each other brothers. They were supposed to go to college together so they could play football and stay that way. Always.

"Anyway. Doesn't matter what he was thinking." Rusty said. "Nothing was gonna change his mind."

The clouds that had gathered on the horizon lit up in a quick series of flashes, revealing vertical streaks of gray below them. I instinctively counted the seconds in my head for the thunder, but it must've been too far away to hear.

Rusty leaned forward, his arms over the front seat, and let out a low whistle. "Looks like we're in for a little storm."

"It's pretty far off, isn't it?"

He leaned forward even farther, straining to look out the windshield. "Right now it is. But it's coming this way fast." As if on cue, the clouds flashed bright again, and this time, after a few seconds, I thought I heard the rumble of thunder over the steady engine of the Pala.

"You want me to drive?" Rusty asked.

I gripped the wheel a little tighter and looked straight

ahead. "No. Thanks. I know how to drive in the rain."

One fat raindrop plopped on the windshield, and almost instantly, a smattering of them followed in quick succession. I reached for the wipers, and another cloud lit up in front of us, electricity zapping a jagged wire of light through it. "Whoa!" I yanked my foot from the gas.

Rusty leaned in close. "Easy, easy. Don't slam the brakes. You're fine. Just let 'er slow down and get your lights on."

I pulled the knob next to the steering wheel and the lights came on, but they didn't make much difference in the strange false-dark that the clouds had brought with them. Way up ahead of us I saw another set of taillights come on just as a flash zipped through the clouds again, lighting them up pink. The crack of thunder that followed drowned out the Pala's engine and boomed in my chest. And then the clouds above us cut loose all the water in them.

I rubbed at the fogged-up windshield in front of me. "Maybe I should pull over. It's getting hard to see."

"Nope. Don't pull over," Rusty said. "Best way to cause an accident. Or end up in a ditch. Just slow down and keep going. Here." He climbed over the front seat, got himself settled, and slid the defrost knob to full blast. "That should help." Hot air rushed in. "Crack your window too, so we don't bake in here."

I did, then concentrated on the road and let out the breath I must've been holding. For the first time since we'd left, I was actually relieved he was there. The fogginess on the windshield disappeared in splotches above the vents at first, while the wipers squeaked a busy rhythm back and forth. Mildly cool air flowed in from the windows, and I breathed in the smell of wet asphalt and dirt that came along with it. I smiled over at Rusty. "Thanks. I don't know why that freaked me out so much. I—"

Brilliant light ripped through the sky above us a split second before the crack of thunder that drowned out every other sound in the world. Rain hammered down even harder, in streams of water the wipers didn't stand a chance against. Through them, all I could see was a blur of jagged lightning and streaky gray.

"Crap!" I lifted my foot from the gas and strained forward against the steering wheel for the lines on the road. "This is crazy. I can't see *anything*." But as I said it, I did see. Two red taillights right in front of us.

I slammed the brakes, and the Pala fishtailed across the highway. The steering wheel jerked wildly in my hands until I couldn't tell if we were sliding or spinning. I froze. Braced myself. Rusty yelled something. Time slowed down, and I got that feeling again like none of it was real. Like there was no way we could be screeching through the rain in Finn's car. Like I wasn't just about to finish off the last of my family, and Rusty too. I braced myself for the end. And then I felt Rusty's weight leaned over on me, his hands on the wheel with mine. He was yelling something I couldn't understand at first, and then I did and yanked my hands from the wheel. Rusty turned it hard once, twice, three times. And then we plowed smack into something big. The force of it threw my chest right into the steering wheel and knocked the wind out of me. I heard another thud that must've been Rusty hitting the dash, and then everything went eerie-quiet, except for the rain that beat down angry against the roof.

11

I brought a trembling hand to my chest. Reached the other one across the seat for Rusty. Lightning flashed above us, and his hand wrapped around mine. "H—you all right?" The smack of the thunder drowned out my attempt at an answer. I took a breath, and pain rippled across my chest. Rusty's hands felt their way up my arm until they found my cheeks, and then he was right there, looking me in the face with clear, worried eyes. "You okay? Say something. You hurt?"

A thin trickle of blood made a line down his temple from somewhere up in his hair, and I watched it, barely able to breathe.

"Honor."

His voice, firmer this time, brought my eyes back to his, and I nodded.

"You okay?"

I nodded again, trying to answer, but my eyes went back to the blood on his cheek, and what little composure I had crumbled. I buried my face in my hands and sobbed. For all of it. For almost killing us, for the blood on Rusty's forehead, for taking off in Finn's car on a stupid trip . . . for the Pala being the only thing I had left of anything, because my parents were dead and my brother was dead and—

Rusty scooted closer and turned the car off. I hadn't even realized it was still running. "Hey, hey. It's okay. We're all right." I heard him suck in a deep breath, and he wrapped a solid arm around my shoulder.

I rested my head back on his arm and looked up at the tiny dots in the upholstery on the ceiling. "I shouldn't have slammed the brakes. You said two seconds before that not to slam the brakes." I looked over at him and brought a shaky hand to the blood moving down his temple. "I almost killed us."

He grabbed my hands and squeezed. "That car came outta nowhere. Anybody would've done that. We're fine, okay?"

I felt my shoulders relax a bit.

He sat back up and looked through the windshield. "Can't say the same for Pala, though. I think we knocked something loose in there."

I sat up and saw a faint but steady stream of something white rising from beneath the hood, up through the rain. "Is that *smoke*? Oh my god, should we get out and check it?" Lightning flickered, followed by a loud rumble.

"No." He rolled down the passenger window and leaned out, stretching toward the hood for a second. When he ducked back in, he was soaked through, the blood washed clean from his face. "Doesn't smell like smoke. I think it's steam."

"What does that mean?"

"That means we're not goin' anywhere for now. Not till it clears up and I can get a look in there." He rolled his window back up, leaving it open just a crack. "We're off the road, from what I can tell, and whatever we hit wasn't that car, but I can't see anything out there. Better sit tight."

I looked out into the gray for some point of reference but couldn't make out anything except the steady sheet of rain that now fell around us. We weren't exactly flush with choices.

Rusty wrapped an arm around my shoulders again, pulling me in a little. "That got a little wild there, but we're fine. All right?"

I drew in a deep breath that was still wobbly with leftover adrenaline. But I believed him. It baffled me how much I did. And it made me wanna cry all over again, because Finn was the only other person in the world I believed like that. And when that soldier came and told me my brother was dead, I didn't think anyone could make me feel like anything could be all right, ever. I sat up and swallowed the lump in my throat, trying to figure out a way to tell Rusty all this.

He held my eyes, and a question knit his brows together. "What?"

I looked into my lap. "Nothing. You just . . . you reminded me of Finn just then." It sounded silly to say it out loud, but I went ahead anyway, eyes focused on my seat-belt buckle. "The way you made everything seem like . . . like it's okay." I smiled as best I could when I looked back up at him. "He was good at that, you know?" My hand went to his knee.

"Anyway. You are too." Rusty's eyes flicked to my hand, and I took it away just as quickly as I'd set it there.

"Glad you think so." He pulled his arm out from behind my shoulder and leaned back against the door, clearly separating that tiny previous moment from the present one. "But Finn was like that all the way through." He looked at the ceiling, letting the thought linger a moment. "The rest of us—we just look that way sometimes." He sighed and reached into his back pocket, then pulled out a small pewter flask. "Anyway." He unscrewed the cap and held it out to me with a smile that was more sad than happy. "You thirsty?"

One sip of whatever he had in there was enough to make me wonder if the old man in the gas station was actually some sort of guardian angel. I washed the burn down with a long gulp of water from the jug and sat back against the seat. The thunder and lightning weren't directly overhead anymore, but every few seconds the sky flashed in a different place, and I could hear the low rumble of the thunder. In between, the rain kept at it, a steady shower that blended into the background like static.

Rusty took up his post stretched out in the backseat again, and I did the same in the front, with my back leaned against the driver-side door and my legs across the seat. We sat there quiet, and the seriousness of the situation slowly settled over me.

"This might be the stupidest thing I've ever done," I said finally.

Rusty took a swig from his flask and swallowed hard. "What? Banged up Pala?"

"No, I mean this whole trip. Going to the concert. Taking off. Missing orientation." I looked at Rusty. "It's selfish, isn't it? Even if he did get me those tickets." He didn't answer, and I took that to mean he agreed.

I brought my eyes to the streaky window, not wanting to cry again, but awfully close. "I just wanted to do something for him, you know? Something big and crazy, like he would have done. And when he cracked that joke about telling Kyra Kelley about him, I just thought . . ." I shook my head at the ridiculousness of it. "I don't know what I thought. I don't even know what I'd tell her if I actually got a chance, or why she'd care. It was a crazy thing to think." I laughed flatly. "Especially now that I got us stuck out here in a ditch and broke the one thing that *did* mean something to him. Stupid."

Rusty pushed himself up against the opposite door so we were facing each other. "Runs in the family, then." I just looked at him. "I mean, your brother did some stupid shit for you back in the day, is all." Rusty took another swallow from his flask and held it out to me.

I shook my head and he sat back against the door, a slow smile on his face. "Best one was gettin' you your prom dress when you went with that skinny little cowboy."

"The red one? Gina got that for me."

"No—Finn got it. I was with him. He drove our asses all the way to Odessa to get it. Twice. The second time, he brought that cowboy kid, too, and made him try it on." I must've looked confused, because Rusty laughed. "He never told you that one, huh?"

"No. He made Steven try on my *dress*?"

Rusty sat up and leaned his arms on the front seat, ready

to fill me in. "Shit," he said, laughing. "I can't believe he never told you." He cleared his throat, but the smile didn't move from his face. "It was all because you came home cryin' about how you couldn't find that dress anywhere and it was all so unfair and you hated living here—all that crap. Gina wasn't havin' it, and you came all undone about it, and so he called all over the place to see if anyone had the dress you wanted. And they had two of them. In Odessa. So he got me up early and we drove out there, and sure thing, they were there." Rusty paused and smiled, and his story hung there like a surprise gift. It made me smile as he went on.

"Only . . . genius had no idea what size you were, couldn't get ahold of you or Gina to ask, and the girl wouldn't hold 'em. So, first we walked around the mall looking for someone your size to try 'em on, but nobody would do it. And then I made some crack about your little date, and Finn got all excited, and we drove all the way back to school and yanked ol' Steve outta practice—"

"Why didn't you guys just come get me?"

Rusty shook his head. "You know how he was. He had it in his head by then that it needed to be a surprise. Besides. You and Steve were built about the same back then, so . . ." I crossed my arms and tried not to smile, because it was kind of true. Although I would've hated Rusty for saying it then.

"So it worked out just fine. We drove all the way back to Odessa and figured out you and Stevie were a size two, you got your dress, and we didn't have to listen to you cry about it anymore."

I smiled at this new story of my brother. It sounded like him. And like Rusty, to have gone along with it. He was the one person Finn never had to ask twice for anything. He held my eyes a moment, then laughed, and I did too. It felt good to talk about Finn that way. Together. After a second, though, it kind of trailed off into the sound of the rain on the roof. I looked down and fiddled with the seat belt.

Rusty leaned back and took another drink from his flask. "Yeah. There's a lot of stupid things your brother talked me into." His eyes slid over to me. "And now you. Carrying on the family tradition."

"I didn't talk you into anything. You passed out in my car."

"You kept driving." That smirk again.

I smiled. "I know. Stupid."

"This'll work out just fine too. The rain'll stop soon and Pala won't be too banged up, and we'll keep going." He shrugged. "Or maybe we won't. Doesn't matter. He woulda liked your crazy-ass idea, anyway."

"Yeah?" I smiled. "I bet he would've liked that you came along for the ride."

Rusty nodded vaguely and looked out the window. "Maybe so. Jury's still out on that one."

We got cozy. Not cozy like close to each other, but cozy like when it's pouring rain out and you're in the house all warm and safe, and you could sit there forever, watching it stream down the windows in wavy little rivers. It was that kind of feeling sitting in Finn's car, with its old vinyl smell all around us and the rain drumming down steadily outside. Rusty and I lay stretched out in each of our seats, passing the last of our road snacks back and forth.

I shook the sour powder from the bottom of the Skittles bag into my palm and licked it off. "There was a lot of stuff you and Finn did together that I never knew about, huh?"

"I guess so." Rusty shrugged. "Bet you didn't tell him everything either."

I rolled the remaining sugar granules on the roof of my mouth, thinking about it, then swallowed. "No, not *everything*.

But you guys had secrets together that started a long time ago." I could remember exactly when. "It was third grade," I said. "That summer after you guys finished third grade and I just got out of second. That was the summer you guys dropped me for each other and stopped telling me things."

Rusty looked at me like he was surprised, or maybe he just knew there was more coming.

"Yep. Girls hold on to those things. That was the first summer you guys didn't let me ride bikes down to the creek with you or go to your rope swing or camp out in the backyard or *anything*." I was a little surprised at how all my seven-year-old indignation came rushing back, clear as day. But up until then, the three of us had been like a team. We did everything together—me working my hardest to keep up with what the boys were doing and them slowing down just enough to let me. Next to my parents dying, which I hardly remembered, Finn and Rusty deciding I couldn't be a part of it anymore was the most traumatic thing that had happened in my short little life.

"I don't remember any of that," Rusty said.

"Course you don't. You weren't the one left behind cryin' while your brother and the friend who used to play Barbie-Legos with you ran off together and said you couldn't come because you were too little. And a girl."

"Barbie-Legos?"

"Yes, Barbie-Legos. You played it with me if Finn was doing something you didn't want to do. You'd bring all your Lego guys over to my Barbie house, and they'd have pool parties and barbecues together." I paused, remembering something else. "And your Lego guys were always trying to get my Barbies to go skinny-dipping."

Rusty nearly spit out his sunflower seeds. "Maybe I do remember that," he said, laughing.

"And then you guys ditched me." I tried to keep from smiling, to see if I could emphasize just how broken up I'd been to be kicked out of the boys' club, but the thought of him sitting there with me and my Barbies was too funny not to.

Rusty put a hand to his chest. "My apologies, then. For trying to get your dolls naked and then ditching you for your brother."

"Thank you," I said solemnly. "Maybe one of these days I'll get over both."

We were quiet a moment, and the sound of the rain grew louder. Rusty leaned his head back against the window and looked over at me. "You know, you can't blame it *all* on me."

"Blame what?"

"That you didn't hang around us later on. I tried, in tenth grade, to keep you around."

I sat up. "What're you talking about?"

Rusty popped a few sunflower seeds in his mouth and grinned. "I told Finn I was gonna take you to homecoming."

"You did not." I leaned over the seat, all kinds of interested to hear about this.

"I did. You were cute that year. Probably why he told me no."

That year . . . as opposed to now? I wanted to say something snappy back, but in a strange way, I was too flattered that he'd thought so. Rusty was the only other sophomore besides Finn on varsity that year, and when they'd come home after practice, I'd made sure I was around. Maybe pass through the kitchen in short shorts, acting like I couldn't care less that Rusty was there. But I'd thought he was cute that year too. Until after homecoming, when I heard he hooked up with this slutty senior girl in the backseat of the Pala. Then I tried to boycott riding in it for a little while out of principle, but it was too far to walk to school. Instead I settled on making a big show of disinfecting it in front of Finn and Rusty, to make sure they knew the depth of my disgust.

"Guess Finn knew what he was doing, telling you no," I said. "We *all* knew what you were doing with Melanie Sloan that night."

Rusty shook his head, smiling. "Melanie Sloan. She smelled like cigarettes and Sour Apple Pucker."

"Nasty."

"Yeah," Rusty mused, "but in a good kind of way."

"Oh my god. You . . ."

He just grinned at me, and we were right back there, in high school, when he was Finn's best friend who alternately intrigued and repelled me. We sat for who knows how long like this, kids camped out, waiting for the rain to let up, swapping stories about Finn and eating through my candy supply while the rain streaked the sky gray outside. There, in our own little world, with Finn as the link between us, we let our guards down, enough to really laugh together.

So when the sun finally did come out, I was more than a little disappointed it had to end. Rusty was the first one to swing open the door and bring us back to reality. He stood stretching in the moisture-thick air, arms high above his head, and I caught myself looking a few seconds too long at the thin line of stomach that showed between his raised shirt and low-slung jeans.

The little jolt it sent through my stomach startled me, and I got out quickly, glancing around for something else to focus my attention on. From the looks of it, we'd zigzagged off the road and skidded through the mud until a cactus, one of those tall, prongy, two-armed ones, stopped us. I shook my hair off my face, and hopefully the blush out of my cheeks, and walked over to examine the cactus. It leaned to the side, like a person who'd had one too many drinks, and I felt a little bad about the scar the Pala's bumper was sure to leave.

Except for the sound of a pickup drifting by on the highway, the rainwashed desert was as still and quiet as could be. Rusty popped the hood with a dull *thunk*, and we both walked over to survey the engine. What we'd be looking for I had no idea, but I figured he would. And I was right. He went straight for the radiator cap, testing it for heat first out of instinct, though it'd long since cooled. As soon as he opened it up, I knew we were in for it.

"Damn," he said, taking a closer look. "It's bone dry in there."

"What's that mean?"

"Means all that steam was the water getting out somewhere." He leaned over the radiator, inspecting it. "Could be a crack. A hose. A slow leak. This been running low on water before now?"

I hesitated, reluctant to admit I hadn't really kept up so well on all those little details in the last few months. "I don't think so. Nothing I noticed."

Rusty rested a forearm on the raised hood, considering the engine. "We're gonna need that water you got."

I went back to the cab and grabbed the almost-full jug,

silently thanking the old minimart guy yet again. "You think this'll last us?" I asked, handing it over.

"We'll see." He tipped it in and let half the water glug into the radiator before capping it. "Like I said, worse comes to worse, we stop off at my mom's." Before I could reply or ask a question, he brought the hood down firmly and headed to the driver's side, dangling the half-empty water jug in his hand. All cool and aloof again, in a way that made me kind of wanna get his attention back. I didn't move from the hood. Just stood there trying to figure out how we'd gone from so easy and comfortable in the car back to . . . this way.

"Hey, Rusty?" I wanted to tell him thank you . . . or that I was really happy he was here . . . or—

"Yeah?" He said it over his shoulder, didn't even bother to turn around as he headed for the driver's side, and somehow that one tiny thing brought my senses back.

"I'm driving," I said. That got him to turn around. "You've been drinking. Out of your little flask thingy." I waved an invisible one between my thumb and forefinger.

He blinked once, twice, then tossed me the keys. "Fine. Just watch the brakes. And the temperature gauge. It starts climbin', we got a problem."

13

Half an hour down the road, we had a problem.

"It's going up—the temperature gauge. Past where it usually is," I said, squinting at the shaking needle.

Rusty leaned over close; so close I could smell the mix of gum and alcohol and whatever deodorant he was wearing. "Damn." He slid the heater knob over to the little red bars, then turned the vents on high. Hot, sticky air blasted out at us.

"What're you *doing*? It's a hundred degrees in here already." I reached to turn it off, but Rusty blocked my hand.

"Leave it. It'll help cool the engine down."

"No, it *won't*. That's not gonna do anything but make it more miserable hot than it already is in here." I had no idea if it would help or not, but the last thing I wanted right then was the heater on full blast. I leaned forward on the wheel and felt the wetness of my tank top cling to my back. "Seriously. Turn that off." I reached for it again.

"We got about forty miles of nothing between here and Sedona, half a jug of water, and a leaking radiator," Rusty said, kicking off his boots. "Give it a few minutes. If it doesn't work, you can turn it off." He leaned back in the seat and stretched out his legs, then locked his fingers behind his head. "It'll work, though."

"Fine." I sighed loud enough for him to hear, unstuck my legs from the seat, and tried to distract myself from the thick, nasty heat. Rusty, with his bare feet down by the door, didn't look half as bothered by it as me, and I wished I'd thought to take my boots off before we got on the road. I briefly contemplated my slip-them-off-while-driving move, but didn't wanna chance landing us off the road again, so I settled on flying an arm out the window instead.

With the heater blasting in the postmonsoon mugginess, and only the Navajo Nation radio station, which was broadcast in Navajo, we were in for a long forty miles. Rusty had gone back to his former self and wasn't much for conversation. But after a few minutes that felt more like a few hours, I gave it a try anyway.

"So, we're gonna stop at your mom's, then?" I said lightly.

Rusty nodded.

"She'll probably be happy to see you, huh? Or have you seen her a lot since you've been at school? Flagstaff's not that far from Sedona, right?"

He let me get out all my questions before he answered. "Nah, it's pretty close. I don't see her a lot, though."

"Oh." I glanced down at the temperature gauge, which had actually fallen a tiny bit. I wished I could feel the difference, even a little. I pulled my hair around to one side to get it off my neck. "Well . . . that's good, right? That you're seeing her and all? Because for so long . . ." I didn't know how to finish this one off. *For so long she hadn't seemed to care, or want to, or try?* "I mean—"

"Yeah, it's good. We're good." He shrugged, then leaned over to check the gauge again. "Damn. Shouldn't be that high still. You better pull over."

I did, and once we were stopped on the shoulder, I could see a thin wall of steam rising from the front and sides of the hood.

"This, though, is *not* good," Rusty said, eyeing it. He swung the door open and in one quick motion pulled his shirt over his head as he got out. I looked—okay, stared this time—at him just standing there, all . . . shirtless. Then I fumbled with my seat belt, wondering how I'd been so pissed at him back at the campsite that I didn't notice how broad his shoulders had gotten or how defined his—

Rusty ducked down and caught my eye. "You gonna turn it off now?"

"The car? Oh—yeah. I was just . . ." *Checking you out?* I cut the engine and sat there a second after he walked to the hood, wondering what the heck had just happened in me to make me see him *that* way. Rusty. Finn's best friend. Who was now shirtless, with his sandy hair grown out just enough to look like he didn't care, and a stomach and set of shoulders that said he did. *Oh, my good lord.* In one of Gina's little pamphlets she'd brought home from the hospital, it listed all sorts of ways grief could affect a person, and it *had* said something about irrational thoughts, but I was pretty sure this wasn't what it was talking about.

I got out of the car, hoping for a little relief from the blasting heater and from my momentary slip into craziness. A cool breeze would be good. Something. But the air hung still and heavy as Rusty wrapped his shirt around his hand and reached for the radiator cap.

"You're not s'posed to—" I backed away to avoid the boiling water that was about to come bursting out. Rusty slowly turned the cap and I heard a hiss of air, but that was it. I took a step forward again. "There's no water in there?"

He leaned over but kept his distance. "Barely. It's leakin' pretty fast."

I looked both directions, up and down the highway, at nothing but shrubby desert and windswept sky. "Can we make it on the rest of that water? To your mom's? And then fix it in time? We have to make it to that concert." Panic rose in my throat. Despite my doubts about going, it was still the only thing I had to hold on to at the moment. "Can we?"

Rusty sighed and ran a hand through his hair. "Maybe. We can put it in, run the heater, and cross fingers it's enough to get there." He looked over at me. "Unless you got a better idea. Or a phone."

"Uh . . ."

I didn't have any better ideas. I did have a phone, but it was useless, considering I hadn't charged it in two days. On the other hand, the thought of running that heater on high for the next thirty miles made me wanna cry. And the water—I was so thirsty all of a sudden. "Maybe we should put *most* of the water in but save some to drink in case we get stuck out here or something."

Rusty thought about it a moment. "Nah. We need every spare drop in Pala. Get a good drink and the rest goes in. We'll make it. I'll drive."

"What—why? You—"

"I'm fine, H. Trust me. You drive her a little hard, is all, and right now she needs to be babied." He gave the car a pat.

I rolled my eyes. Finn used to tell me that same thing, and I never understood what he meant by "driving hard," especially when I didn't see any difference in the way he drove it from the way I did. But fine. We needed to get going, and I was too hot to stand there arguing. And the driver's side was hotter on your feet anyway. I went and grabbed the jug, took a good, long gulp of unrefreshing, car-warmed water, and passed it to Rusty, who did the same. Then we both watched as he poured every last drop into the radiator and capped it.

"Here goes nothin'," he said.

He shut the hood, and I walked to the passenger door, eager to get my feet out of my boots. The relief was immediate when I did, and I leaned back in the seat with my eyes closed, trying to spread the feeling over the rest of me. I heard Rusty walk over to the driver's side and waited to feel the seat bump when he sat down and settled in.

Instead, I heard a zipper.

I opened one eye and turned my head just in time to see Rusty standing behind the driver's door, pulling his jeans down. "*What* are you doing?" I sat up and looked around, like I shouldn't be seeing him or like someone else might see me see him and know how instantly hot it made my cheeks.

Rusty didn't answer. He was bent over, trying to get his foot out of one of his pant legs.

"What are you *doing*? You *are* drunk. Gimme the keys."

He finally got the one foot out, then stood on it and pulled his jeans off the other leg. Then he bunched them up and threw them in the backseat, sat down behind the wheel so hard I bounced, and looked at me like I was the ridiculous one. "I'm not drunk. It's hotter than shit, we got a ways to go, and I'm sweatin' balls."

I didn't really have a response for that.

Except to burst out laughing. And then try to compose myself while Rusty looked at me, completely straight-faced, which brought on another wave. He just sat there in his faded plaid boxers, waiting patiently for me to finish.

I sucked in a big breath of air, cleared my throat, and did my best to mirror his straight face. "So . . . you're just gonna . . . drive in your underwear. Because it's hot. And you're . . . *sweating balls*." I pressed my lips together and nodded like it was totally reasonable.

"Pretty much." He turned the key, then adjusted the mirrors back to his liking. "Wouldn't bother me if you did, too."

I laughed again and looked out my window, far away from Rusty in his underwear. Tan, built Rusty, who was now grinning at the dare like there wasn't a chance I'd do it.

"Oh, yeah?" I stalled, doing a quick mental check of my guts and what I had on under my clothes.

He shrugged. "It'd be fine."

I watched him for a second, trying to see if there was any hint of anything coming from him. And then I chickened out. "Thanks. I'm good, though." I let my eyes shift ever so slightly in his direction when he looked over his shoulder and pulled us back onto the highway.

"Suit yourself," he said casually. He caught my eyes for a second, then grinned confidence down the road. "Just try not to stare too hard."

14

I never wanted to take my clothes off so badly in my entire life. After three spurts of driving, with three stops in between to let the engine cool down, my tank top was so sweat soaked, I'd given up unsticking it from myself. And my cutoffs. Well. They were a lost cause, no matter how I sat. I glanced over at Rusty, who looked relaxed and relatively comfortable, like he was catching a nice breeze for his, um . . . problem.

I'd run out of things to talk about that didn't have to do with how miserable hot I was, and decided it was probably best to keep my mouth shut anyway, because I was a little scared I might say something embarrassing. So I sat quiet, alternating between trying to figure out how to sit so that the least amount of me was touching the seat, and making a concerted effort not to look over at him in his underwear. Too much. Rusty didn't seem to notice the craziness that was going on in my mind. He drove and watched the temperature needle like the world depended on it. Which it kinda did.

He shook his head. "Thing's way too hot. We need more water."

"You could pour the rest of your whiskey in there." I meant it as a joke, but it came out sarcastic.

Rusty didn't respond.

I bent forward and rummaged around the floor until I found the two things I was looking for—my soda cup, which now held a brown-tinged mix of melted ice and the last drops of Coke, and the plastic soda bottle from the day before, still two-thirds of the way full and hot. I held them up to Rusty. "What about these?"

He slid his eyes over and took in what I was offering, then lit up a little. "Couldn't hurt. We still got about twenty miles, and I bet that thing's dry again." He slowed, and we bumped over the dirt and gravel before coming to a stop. When he cut the engine, the Pala shuddered off, then was still. No sounds of bubbling water or steam or anything.

Rusty patted the dash. "Come on, Peaches. We only gotta make it a few more miles. Hang in there."

"Peaches?"

He ignored me.

Normally, I would've given him a hard time for this. I always did with Finn whenever he started talking about the Pala like it was a girl. It was another one of those things I never got, and the couple of times I teased Finn about it, he just grinned his happy grin at me and brushed it off. Now I understood it was probably another joke between him and

Rusty that I wasn't in on, and chose to ignore it. I got out of the car, grateful for a little air.

Rusty did too, even though he was in his underwear. It was funny the first time we stopped, and every time after that, it made my cheeks rush hot all over again. By now he treated it as routine, as if it were normal to do all these things in your underwear: Get out, stretch, look over miles of desert that didn't change, check the engine, get honked at and flashed by a car full of girls zooming by with their music blaring. None of it fazed him. Which was kind of even more attractive. Oh, god. I could barely stand myself.

I looked across the barren flatness to the mountains I hoped we'd make it to. I was sick of flat, ugly desert. I could've stayed in Texas to see this much brown dirt. But Finn had told me to go on an adventure, put my feet in the ocean. He'd set me down the highway with a pair of tickets and made it seem important enough to blow off orientation week and lie to Aunt Gina, not that he'd had any idea I'd do those things. I was having a hard time believing it myself. Guilt tugged at me again, heavy with the fear that I'd just used Finn's gift as an excuse to run away. That even as I told myself I was doing this for him, it was a selfish thing. Maybe this ugly desert and broken-down car were fate's way of telling me so. I motioned at the shrubs in front of us, wanting to change the subject in my mind. "Does Sedona look like this too?"

Rusty leaned against the passenger door, next to me. "No. It's not like this. It's real pretty. All red rocks and blue sky. You'll like it."

"And your mom won't mind us staying?" Rusty shook his

head. "And you can fix the car? Because I don't think I have enough money—"

"We'll get it fixed."

"And then we'll keep going? To California?"

"Wherever you want."

"Rusty?"

"Yeah?" He looked at me this time, with hazel eyes that were familiar—and not—at the same time.

"Thank you," I said. "I'm glad you're here." I pushed a stray strand of hair behind my ear, feeling like I was teetering on the edge of some kind of moment I wasn't sure about, so I stood up straight and steered us away from it with a grin. "Even if you do stink and your underwear needed to be replaced about two years ago." I looked down at them pointedly this time, motioning at the hole in the seam at his hip.

A slow smile spread out across his face, into a laugh. "You're probably right," he said, turning to face me. He reeled his laugh back into a smile, then leaned in close and almost whispered. "But that shirt you're sweatin' through?" He glanced down casually, and I felt every inch his eyes passed over. "It's pretty bad too." He raised his eyebrows, then grabbed the sodas off the roof and headed to the hood of the car.

I looked at the sun hanging low in the sky but didn't feel the slightest hint of coolness. Thought of getting back into the blast of the Pala's heater. And then decided: What the hell? I did it quick so I wouldn't chicken out again—grabbed the bottom of my tank top and pulled it over my head, surprised at the immediate relief of having it off my skin. Then I shimmied out of my shorts and threw them in the back like Rusty had done with his jeans. And I stood there in my bra and underwear, feeling on my skin the softness of the breeze, which made me happier than anything so far that day.

Rusty finished pouring out the last bit of soda into the radiator, capped it, and shut the hood. When he turned to come back, he stopped short and did a double take. Then he smiled slow, nodded once, and got in without saying anything. What did that mean? Was I being ridiculous? *Oh, god, what was I* thinking? I stood there, trying to collect myself and work up the nerve to get in the car, just as cool as he had. It was just underwear, just like a bathing suit. And it was only Rusty. Except that my underwear was black and lacy. And Rusty was good looking as all get-out.

He leaned over to the passenger side. "You comin'? Or you get all undressed to try and hitch your own ride?"

I took a deep breath and mustered every bit of confidence I could. Then I slid into the seat, shut the door, and looked over at Rusty like this was something I did all the time. "Nah. I think I'll stick with you, at least for a little while." *Oh, god. Ridiculous.*

He didn't move. Just sat there looking at me, quite amused, and I knew I was in for some joke at my expense. Instead, he just shook his head, still smiling. "Shit. You."

"What? You said it wouldn't bother you." No response. "It's still hotter than hell." Now I was getting defensive. He turned the key, and the Pala sputtered to life. "Why are you acting all weird about it?"

Rusty glanced in the side mirror, then put the car in gear and pulled us back on the highway. "I'm not. You're . . ." He smiled like he was gonna laugh. I reached for my clothes, feeling every kind of embarrassed I possibly could.

"Oh, c'mon. Leave 'em. You're fine." His eyes flicked over in my general direction.

"Well, then," I said, confidence bolstered. "Try not to stare too hard, all right?" My voice, and what it said, surprised the heck out of me.

Even Rusty seemed surprised. He laughed the kind of laugh you do when you don't know what to say, then reached for the radio knob. "Duly noted."

Before any kind of awkward silence could settle over us, the static gave way to one of *my* all-time favorites. I leaned forward and turned the volume up, got the tuning just right so it came in clear. Then I sat back, feeling the hot wind on my bare skin, and right along with Tom Petty belted out the chorus of "Free Fallin'." And it was the perfect song for what I felt that moment.

Because in a lot of ways, I was.

15

The last of the heavy sun dipped behind red-rock mountains, splashing brilliant pink light over the clouds that streaked the sky, and I wished I could capture that moment right there, remember how perfectly peaceful it felt. We'd chugged along slowly since we put the soda in the radiator, and I'd lost my senses enough to take off my clothes. The giggly nervousness (mine) and sneaky glances (both of us), I thought, had given way to a silence between Rusty and me that was comfortable as the day finally began to cool. The twilight spread out and deepened as we drove, enough for Rusty to flick on the headlights. The beams swung around a wide curve in the road, and on the other side of it he let out a long sigh. "That's it, right down the hill. Almost there."

In front of us, nestled down between the silhouettes of

towering cliffs, were the first twinkling lights of Sedona. A wave of relief and happiness hit me so strong I nearly started crying. "Oh my god. We really made it." I sat up and looked out the windshield, wondering where his mom's house was. The prospect of a home with food and a shower was just about the best thing I could imagine at the moment.

"You think your mom'll mind if the first thing I do when we get there is take a shower?" I was almost giddy with the thought.

Rusty laughed. "She might wanna say hi first."

"I know *that*." I smacked his bare thigh before I thought about it, and he raised an eyebrow, which I chose to ignore. Then the lightness drained from me almost in an instant when I thought about seeing her and having to face the inevitable conversation about Finn. I looked over at Rusty, afraid to ask. "Does she know? About him?"

His jaw tightened when he nodded. "Yeah—" He glanced over at me, then back at the road. "She's the one who told me." I opened my mouth to ask where she'd heard, or how, or why she'd been the one to tell him, but I didn't get a chance to pick out the right question before Rusty slowed the Pala and turned us onto an unmarked dirt road. "House is out here a little ways," he said. "Might wanna put your clothes on. Bru'll probably be there."

"Bru?"

Rusty leaned forward on the wheel. "Her boyfriend. It's his house."

"Boyfriend?" There were turning out to be all kinds of things I had no idea about. I looked over at Rusty through the dusky light, trying to add it all up, but he didn't look like he was going to help me out. "How long have they been together?" I asked.

"I don't know. A while."

"Well . . . do you *like* him?"

"He's all right."

We bumped over the dirt, kicking up dust that glowed peachy in the headlights. I watched Rusty carefully, thinking he had to have been here more than a few times to find the road we were on. Maybe I'd been wrong this whole time, thinking that he and his mom didn't talk or that he was still angry and hurt over her leaving.

"What's he like?" I asked, trying to figure out how he felt about this boyfriend of his mom's.

"I don't know. Like a crusty old mountain guy who's dating my mom."

There, at least, was a sort-of answer. Which only brought up more questions in my mind. "Is he a good guy?" I asked. "I mean . . . is he good to her?"

He looked over at me quick, then put his eyes back on the road, which was now climbing a steep hillside. "Better'n my dad. If that's what you mean."

I hadn't *really* meant it that way, but the simple truth of his answer and the fact that he said it out loud shocked me quiet. I never knew his parents real well, but I knew about them. Or . . . knew what went around the town rumor mill about them. Nobody was surprised when she up and left. What did surprise people, though, was that she left Rusty behind with his dad's booze-fueled temper and his tendency to take it out on whoever was closest.

I could remember being little, seeing his parents in the bleachers at elementary school football games. I'd always watch the pairs of moms and dads, wondering what mine would've been doing if they'd been there. His parents were the one couple I tried not to watch because his dad was always angry about something, and I felt sorry for his mom. She seemed too delicate and fragile to handle his loud, quick temper. I saw him grab her arm more than once, in a way that made me scared of him and angry at the same time. I could only imagine what it would've been like to be Rusty as a little kid. Or a grown one, for that matter.

All at once, I wanted to be gentle with him. "I didn't mean anything like that," I said softly. "I just wondered what you thought of him."

"I know," Rusty answered. "It's fine."

And I knew, from the shift in his tone, he was about to change the subject. He didn't have to, though, because just then we rounded a curve that ended in a narrow dirt driveway. At the end of it was a house that looked like it had clung to the side of the mountain for years. Once again, I was speechless. But this time, it was because of the view.

Far below, the sparkling lights of Sedona spread out like stars on the valley floor, distant and quiet. And above us, in the moonless purple sky, the real stars felt closer than they'd ever been, like I could reach right up, pluck one from the night, and tuck it in my pocket. It was the kind of sky Finn would've loved. Almost in answer to my thought, a delicate trail of white light streaked low over the horizon.

"You see that?" I asked Rusty.

He nodded. "Make a wish."

Had he said it to me a few hours earlier, I might've wished myself back home or wished that the envelope that contained Finn's letter hadn't been his last. But right then, I felt grateful we'd made it this far and that Rusty was with me. So I wished us all the way to Kyra Kelley.

Neither of us spoke. We just sat there a moment, and relief and exhaustion settled over me. A cool, fragile breeze drifted in the windows, carrying with it the rich, dry smells of the desert. The night outside lay so utterly peaceful, I wanted to sink into it and float off with the scent of the pines. I glanced over at Rusty, who seemed to feel the same way, judging by the way he leaned back against the seat, taking in the night sky.

He felt me looking and gave a half smile. "You ready?" When I nodded, he put the car back in gear and we rolled quietly down the driveway. Rusty pulled in next to a mud-splattered jeep and cut the engine. The Pala seemed to shudder with relief as soon as he did, and everything stood still and quiet until the front door of the house opened up, spilling out orange light and the small, unmistakable frame of Celia.

She moved fluidly down the stairs, jewelry jingling softly as she did, and made her way right to my open window. I sat up, too tired to care that I hadn't seen her in years and I was showing up in my underwear with her son. When she reached the passenger door and bent down to the window, I knew it didn't matter.

She smiled, gentle and warm, took my face in her hands, and said softly, "We've been expecting you."

16

I closed my eyes and let the warm water stream down my face, hoping it would carry any traces of tears away with it. The look on Celia's face, and her hands on my cheeks, and what she'd said, had left me so near undone I actually did ask right away if I could take a shower. And she'd been happy to oblige, because that's what you do with people who are so upset they've lost their manners. I'd barely gotten the water on before the first tears, all full of fatigue and relief, spilled over onto my cheeks. I watched them swirl down the drain, wondering how in the world Celia had been expecting me when I had absolutely no business being where I was at the moment. I probably didn't have enough money to fix the car and make it home, let alone get to California and Kyra Kelley in time. Lilah had to be wondering why I hadn't returned her calls, and Gina probably had all of Texas searching for me, yet here I was.

What felt the worst, though, was that being this far away and this out of touch was exactly what I wanted right now—needed, even, because back home Finn was gone for good. Buried in the town cemetery. But in his car, with Rusty next to me and memories of him shared between us, it was like he wasn't so far away after all.

I breathed in the steam, wishing I could stay in the shower forever and not have to deal with any of it. I could only imagine the conversation happening about me between Rusty and Celia out in the living room. But I actually did remember my manners, and I couldn't let go of my curiosity about how she'd known we were coming, so I finished up and shut the water off, then took a few deep breaths as I put my fresh clothes on. At least I'd be fully dressed to give her a proper greeting and meet Bru.

Which I did, as soon as I swung open the bathroom door. I ran right smack into him in the middle of the hallway, almost knocking both of us down.

"Oh my gosh, I'm so sorry, I didn't see . . . I . . ."

"That's all right, darlin'." He laughed. "You didn't hurt me none."

Rusty hadn't been kidding about the crusty mountain man thing. Bru stood not much taller than me, his faded jeans and western shirt almost completely covered in red-brown dust. He tipped his head and smiled warmly, past his scruffy white beard, all the way up to a pair of sparkly blue eyes. "You must be Honor." He stuck out his hand. "I'm Bru. Pleased to meet you." A scraggly gray ponytail slipped over his shoulder as he leaned forward. "My condolences about your brother."

"Thank you," I said, shaking his hand and hoping he'd

leave it at that. "And . . . thank you for having us here. Sorry to just show up like this, but—"

He waved a dismissive hand. "We're happy to have you two," he said with a wink. "You all done in there? Cece doesn't like me to show up to the table all dusty."

I nodded, still fumbling around for something more to say. "Yeah. I'm finished. Thank you." I stepped aside and motioned that the bathroom was all his.

"All right then. Kitchen's down the hall and through the living room. Just follow the smell of whatever crazy thing she's cookin' in there." He winked again, then stepped past me. "Lord knows what it is this time."

"What *is* that?" Rusty said as I stepped down into the kitchen. Now dressed in a pair of jeans and a T-shirt, he leaned over the pan that sizzled on the stove, face scrunched up at the smell of it.

Celia reached up to his shoulders, which made her look even tinier, and steered him toward one of the kitchen chairs. "*That* is our dinner—organic quinoa with sprouted nuts and leafy kale. You just sit down and don't bother yourself about it now." Rusty did as she said, with a look that said he probably wouldn't bother with it at all.

Celia was about to say something else but noticed me and crossed the kitchen in about two steps, then stood looking me over, shaking her head. "Oh, Honor darlin', look at you all grown. You're every bit as beautiful as your mama was."

I looked down at my toes on the wood floor, a mix of self-conscious and happy at the comparison. "Thank you, ma'am," I said, looking up into her hazel eyes. "You look just the same as I remember you." And she did, with her long curly hair and olive skin that made her look more like she could be Rusty's sister than his mother.

She waved a dismissive hand, then smiled as she brought it to my arm. "Aw, sweetie, I'm just happy you're here. Happy Rus went down there after you. I knew it would work out for the best." My eyes went straight to Rusty, but he didn't meet them, and Celia's sentence hung there in the space between us.

She gave my arm a pat, then turned her attention to the pan on the stove, which was starting to smoke. "Oh, lord!" she said, hurrying over to it.

Went down there after me?

Rusty still wouldn't meet my eyes. I looked to Celia, about to ask her what she meant, but she was too busy fussing over the pan that was now filling the room with putrid-smelling smoke. *Went down there after me . . .* For what? And how did she know that? And why wouldn't Rusty even look at me?

The contents of the pan crackled, then ignited. Celia jumped back with a shriek. Rusty was on his feet and across the kitchen in one quick motion. He grabbed the handle of the pan, threw it in the sink, and spun the faucet on, sending a hiss of steam up like a rocket. I sat glued to my chair in the little swirl of chaos, absorbed by question after question and the unsettling feeling that everyone here knew more than me about something.

Just then, Bru stepped into the kitchen all showered up and smelling like patchouli oil. Enough to compete with the pungent burning smell that now blanketed the room. He took the situation in like it was nothing out of the ordinary, grabbed a set of keys hanging on the hook by the door, and said simply, "I'll go get the pizza, then. Combo okay for everybody?"

I nodded, eyeing Rusty across the kitchen. He smiled at Bru. "That'll be fine."

Celia blew a loose curl off her forehead, smoothed her dress, then smiled a thank-you at him. "You're the best, baby. I don't know what went wrong that time, but one of these days I'll get this whole cooking thing, I will," she said, wiping her hands with a dish towel.

Bru walked over and gave her a quick kiss on the cheek. "Hopefully I'll live to see it." He put his hat on and looked from me to Rusty. "Anybody need anything else while I'm out?"

We were all quiet.

"Okay, then. I'll be back in time for the star show."

17

The "star show," as Bru called it, was enough to make me forget everything else the moment I looked at the sky. When he got home with the pizza, he herded us all out onto the deck. It jutted out over the side of the mountain and left the impression we were floating between the valley and the stars. We settled around a circular wooden table lit by a single candle so we'd have enough light to see, but not so much that it drowned out the light of the falling stars that streaked fast across the sky every few seconds.

"They're called the Perseids," Bru said through a mouthful of pizza. "Because they all look like they come from Perseus up there." I remembered Perseus from English. He was the one who killed Medusa and saved Andromeda and tamed Pegasus—all these impossible things that made him the kind of legend that got his own constellation. Another faint tail of light skimmed over the mountaintops, and I tried to trace its path back to the bigger-than-life hero in the sky.

"All these shooting stars come from the same place?" I asked, searching for the next one.

"Yes and no," Bru answered. He set his slice of pizza down. "They're not really stars, but they do come from the same place. It's a big ol' cloud of comet dust. Little bits of rock and ice no bigger'n the grains of sand on the beach."

I considered this as two more, fainter than the ones before, etched barely visible lines across the black of the sky. It didn't seem possible that something so tiny could make light that we could see all the way down here.

"Just beautiful," Celia whispered.

Rusty leaned forward, elbows on the table, and said exactly what I was thinking. "I don't understand."

Bru thought about it for a second, then turned to face us. "Without gettin' too tricky, it's like this. Every August, the earth's orbit crosses this cloud of debris left behind by a comet that swung by years ago. When those little bits hit our atmosphere and burn up, they put on quite a light show."

I glanced at Rusty and wondered if that's what we were—the little bits left behind to burn up and fall after the bright streak of a comet had come and gone. We'd definitely put on a show the last two days.

We sat eating in silence for a little while, watching the pieces of comet dust flare up and rain down delicate white light. When the box was empty but for one last slice, Bru leaned back in his chair, patting his round little belly. "Somebody's got to finish that off, and it shouldn't be me. Honor . . . Cece?"

"No, thank you," I said. Celia shook her head.

"Rusty?"

"Nah, I'm full." He stretched his arms above his head and yawned. "And I gotta go to bed soon. I wanna be up early to work on the car." He glanced over at me. "We're on a deadline here."

Bru leaned forward and grabbed the piece of pizza. "I can help you out with it after I get back from my a.m. tour. I'll be back early. Some crazy tourist lady booked a *sunrise* Vortex tour. Which means I gotta get up at four to get the jeep ready."

"Bru does jeep tours around the mountains here," Celia explained. She reached around the table for our empty paper plates and unused packets of parmesan cheese and pepper flakes. "The Vortex tours are his most popular ones."

"Vortex?" I asked.

Rusty leaned his head back on the chair and put his face to the sky. "Oh, damn, here we go. Thought we already had our cosmic lesson for the night."

Bru turned his attention to me, ignoring him. "A vortex," he began in his teacherly kind of tone, "is basically a spot where you can feel the energy the earth gives off," he said, crunching his last bite of pizza crust. "But amplified. For reasons we don't really know about. The Indian tribes around here found 'em and used 'em for all their spiritual ceremonies. And now people visit them for all different reasons—meditation, peace, clarity . . . what have you."

He wiped his mouth with a napkin but missed a few crumbs that fell to his beard, and I tried not to watch them move up and down as he talked. "The spots affect everyone different, just depends on what you're there for and how open you are to it." Rusty snorted, but Bru went on unfazed. "They're all over around here, around the whole world, actually, but you gotta know how to find 'em, and that's where I come in."

"So, you take people up to these spots . . . and then what?" I asked. He said it all so matter of factly, I was genuinely curious. Men who wore turquoise jewelry and talked about the earth's energy weren't exactly common in Big Lake, where oil and football were at the top of the accepted list of conversation topics.

"And then they pay him a lot of money and say they're enlightened," Rusty answered.

Bru chuckled. "I don't know about *a lot* of money, but some of 'em do come back with the insight they were looking for."

I nodded like I understood, but I was still a little hazy on how it was supposed to work. Bru waved his hand. "Anyway, that's just work stuff. When I'm done with that, we'll get to work on your car, so don't you worry about it." He stood and patted me firmly on the shoulder. "We'll get her all fixed up tomorrow, and you can be on your way."

"Thank you," I said. "I appreciate it." And I really did. He had a calm about the way he spoke that was reassuring all on its own.

"Sure thing," Bru said with a wink. "See y'all in the mornin'." He pushed himself out of his chair with a grunt, then leaned down and gave Celia another kiss on the cheek and shuffled back into the house, leaving the three of us out there in the cool night air with comet dust falling all around.

After a moment when we were all quiet, I turned to Celia. "Have you gone to one of those places? The vortexes?"

She smiled a warm, soft smile. "I have. They've helped

me work through a lot of things in my life. Met Bru at one of them, as a matter of fact. That's a story for another night, though." She leaned her head back and sighed. Then, after a long moment, said, "We should probably all be getting to bed soon. You two must've had a long day. Probably could use the rest." Neither of us said anything, and I wondered if it had seemed as long to Rusty as it had to me. Watching the sunrise with Wyatt, the fight with Rusty afterward, the monsoon and the car crash, all of it felt like years packed into the space of a day.

Celia lay a soft hand over mine, and I could see out the corner of my eye she put her other one on Rusty's. She breathed in deep and closed her eyes, chin lifted up to the starry sky, and the glow from the candle made her long, soft curls shine gold. "I think that car breaking down on you is a sign," she said dreamily. Rusty shifted in his seat, but she kept her hand on his. "I mean it. I think the two of you are supposed to be here together right now, sharing this."

I glanced over at Rusty, curious if he thought it was crazy, what she'd just said. And also kind of wondering if I was a little crazy for liking that she'd said it.

"Don't get started with all your New Age crap," he said, drawing his hand away. "We're supposed to be to the California state line by now."

Celia sat up. "I'm sorry, honey. It just came out." She turned to me. "Rus doesn't like it when I talk like that. Doesn't believe in his own mama's intuition. But I tell you what—some things are so true you can feel 'em right here." She put her hand to her chest. "And that's one of 'em. You two are meant to be in this together. Here."

She nodded to herself, then her hand went from her chest to my arm. "Which reminds me, Honor, I think it's just perfect that you're taking those tickets Finn gave you and going to see Kyra Kelley. I'm sure he would've wanted you to."

I shot a *thanks a lot* look over at Rusty, but Celia didn't seem to notice. She was too excited right then, her hands all aflutter as she spoke. "Have you been reading about what she's going through, with her boyfriend cheatin' on her and her manager stealing from her and all? That is a girl who needs someone genuine in her life right now!" I looked from Celia to Rusty, who was leaned back into the shadows, trying to hide a smirk. Celia hopped up from her chair. "Matter of fact, I just read an article about her that you need to read for yourself—it was all about how she's at this complete crossroads in her life right now, you know, looking for the right path to take. A lot like you, probably, and . . . I'll just go and get it." Without waiting for a response, she disappeared through the sliding glass door into the house.

I sighed at Rusty, who still hadn't said anything from across the table. "You *told* her about Kyra Kelley?"

"What was I supposed to say we were doin' here?"

"I don't know," I shot back. "Apparently we're *supposed* to be here. Earlier, she seemed to think you went home to get me." I looked at him straight on. "Is that true?"

Rusty stayed quiet, and out of nowhere something in me felt close to breaking down. I looked to the sky for the next shooting star, hoping it might quiet the confusion in my head, but nothing came, and my eyes landed right back on Rusty.

"I don't understand," I said. "I don't understand why she's acting like you came home to get me, or why you would in the first place, because . . ." I paused to breathe, a last grasp at composure before I went on and said what had been in the back of my mind since he showed up in my driveway. "Because the day Finn enlisted, you were so mad at him, and hurt. And I understood. You guys . . . you had it all laid out in front of you—football and college, and you lost all that when he changed his mind. But . . ."—I fumbled with the words on the tip of my tongue before I finally got them out—"but you seemed like you hated *me* for what he decided, like it was *my* fault, and I . . ." I dropped my eyes to a crack in the wood of the table. "I never understood that. At all."

Silence stretched out heavy and hung in the air above us a long time before Rusty spoke. "I never hated you, H." The words were there, but there wasn't a whole lot of reassurance behind them.

I traced the crack in the table, afraid if I looked at him, I'd cry. He sighed and leaned back in his chair. "I've been here since my mom showed up at practice a couple weeks ago and told me Finn was dead. We've been talkin' about a lot of things, and you were one of them."

I felt his eyes on me and met them for a second before looking away again.

"My dad called her with the news about Finn, and she drove over and found me at practice," he said. "As soon as I saw her there I knew it was something. And when she said the words, I just left, just walked off the field and came down here with her to stay awhile." I watched out the corner of my eye as he chewed on his lip for a second and said more to the table than me, "I didn't wanna go back home at first. Didn't wanna go to his funeral, you know? 'Cuz that would mean it was true—that he was really gone, and I . . ."

He didn't finish, and I wanted to take his hand in mine or put my arm around him or just tell him I understood. Because I'd felt the same way. I'd gotten used to Finn being away, and in the time between the day we heard the news and the day of his funeral, I let myself pretend that's what it was, that he was still just . . . away. Even with the sympathy food slowly filling our fridge and the candles and flowers and flags on our front lawn, I still felt like it could be a colossal mistake. That Finn had just gotten lost in the chaos after the blast, one so strong it blew his dog tags right off, made them think the dead soldier they landed near was him. And maybe he'd been surviving out there in the desert, alone but alive, doing everything he could to make it back to his base and let us know he was okay. Denial's a stubborn thing. And necessary at first, so the world doesn't come crashing down on you all at once.

But the day Gina and I stood in the hundred-degree airplane hangar to meet the plane carrying his remains, my world had cracked right down the center. When the plane landed and the door slid open enough to show the shiny, metal casket inside, reality knocked me down so hard, I couldn't breathe. So I understood what Rusty meant.

"Why'd you come, then?" I asked.

Rusty rubbed his forehead. "Because. It was the right thing to do." He took a deep breath and looked right at me. "And because I promised Finn if anything ever happened to him, I'd look out for you."

I stared at him. "When?"

"What do you mean, when?"

"I mean when did you promise him that?"

"I don't know, once he got over there and realized there was a chance. He had a lot of close calls—what does that have to do with anything?"

I opened my mouth to say something, but I didn't know where to begin or which feeling was the right one just then—surprise and hurt and jealousy were all having it out in my chest at the moment. Finn hadn't mentioned to me, in any of his e-mails, that he'd had any close calls or that he and Rusty were talking again. Definitely not that they were talking about me and how I needed to be looked out for in case anything happened to him. And by *Rusty*? Of all people? Anger flared in me, and I felt like I was seven years old all over again, left just outside their tight little circle of friendship.

The screen door slid open and Celia stepped out, rifling through a pile of magazines in her arms. "Okay, I know this looks like a lot, but . . ." Right away she seemed to sense the tension sitting like a wall between us. She looked from me to Rusty and back again, then set the magazines down gingerly. "You know, it's late. Why don't I just leave 'em here, and we can go through them all tomorrow, okay?"

I pulled my eyes away from Rusty's long enough to answer, "Okay . . . thank you." But then I looked right back at him. Hard. "I've just about had enough of this day anyway." I pushed my chair out behind me and tried to temper my voice when I stood and spoke to Celia again. "I think I need to get some sleep."

She looked me over carefully with eyes that wanted to understand, then glanced briefly at Rusty before she put her arm around my shoulder. "All right sweetie. I'll show you to the guest room."

I may have needed sleep, but it didn't come. Not after I heard Celia and Rusty pull out the sofa bed and their whispers before she told him good night. Not after her door clicked shut and the house went quiet. Not even after I heard someone snoring rhythmic and low somewhere in the house. Instead, I lay there on my back in the guest room, with the light turned off so Rusty'd think I was asleep, and the window wide open, spilling in cool night air. I tried to pick out constellations in the sky, patterns that would help me make sense of why I felt so . . . so . . . I didn't even know what it was, but it was enough to keep me balanced on the edge of angry tears all night.

It wasn't that Finn had patched things up with Rusty. *That* I was actually glad to hear. They were best friends. It was just that I hadn't even known, and by the time Finn left and started writing to me, I'd liked the feeling that *I* was the one he kept in touch with and told things to. The one he was closest to. Instead I was the one who still needed protecting, because he didn't believe in me like he said.

My breath hitched as a new thought occurred to me. It wasn't Rusty who had left me out. He was gone to school by then, with no reason to keep in touch with me. It was Finn—my brother—who I should be mad at, who all of a sudden I *was* mad at. Not just for not telling me every little detail of his life but for all of it—enlisting and leaving when he didn't have to, for some stupid reason I didn't understand and he never explained. For dying because of it and not being here now, when I was lost and needed him most.

18

I snapped to attention at the sound of footfalls outside my door. I had no idea what time it was, but I sat up in bed, sure all of a sudden that Rusty had been lying awake on the couch all this time too and was coming to talk to me about things. But nobody knocked. The door didn't ease open. The footsteps went past the door, right down the hallway to the kitchen.

It had to be Bru, then, up for his vortex tour. Which meant it was four a.m., and any hope I had for sleep was probably lost by now. The last thing I wanted to do was lie there waiting for the sun to come up, then have to face Rusty right off the bat. I needed to sort myself out first. Really, if there was anything that would do me some good, it'd be fresh air. A little peace or clarity or whatever Bru had called it couldn't hurt either. I jumped up, still in my clothes, and yanked on my boots just as the jeep's engine rumbled to life outside.

The first step out the door told me it was a good idea. I breathed in the starry coolness of the morning and the potential of a new day, still all crisp and clean in the dark. Bru was leaned over the side of the jeep clanking something around when I made it down the porch steps.

"Can I come? To the vortex?"

He spun around, reaching inside his jacket like a cowboy in the old westerns, then brought his hand to his chest and smiled in recognition at me. "Holy Hell, girl. You tryin' to get shot first thing in the mornin'?"

"I'm sorry. I just heard the engine, and I was hoping . . . Are you really wearing a *gun*?" I squinted at him in the dark.

He patted his side. "Safety precaution. Never know what you might find out there in the dark."

"Oh." I waited a second for the punch line, but he went back to clanking around the jeep, serious as could be. "Um . . . Bru?"

"What's that, darlin'?" he asked, walking around to the driver's side of the jeep.

"Well . . . I was hoping you might have an extra seat. For the vortex thing. I could pay you . . . or be a lookout or something."

Bru chuckled, then motioned at the jeep with a nod. "I got room. And I could use somebody to make nice with the hoity-toity ladies I got booked this mornin'. I'm not at my most charmin' before sunrise." He hoisted himself up into the driver's seat and slammed the door. "Hop on in. Let's go get us some coffee."

By the time we pulled up to the valet area of the swanky resort to pick up Bru's tour ladies, he'd sucked down the whole thermosful of coffee he'd filled up at the minimart. "Cece doesn't keep any coffee in the house," he explained, screwing the silver cup lid back on. "She likes all that herbal tea stuff that doesn't do a dang thing to help you wake up, so I gotta get my fix when I can." He put the jeep in park and cut the engine. "Also helps with the whole charming bit—which I'm gonna need, from the looks of it." He motioned with his head, and my eyes caught what he was talking about.

Coming out of the massive frosted-glass doors of the lobby were two tiny blondes in pink track suits and little bejeweled hats pulled down low. They carried coffee cups and giant purses like all the stars in magazines, and they came out whispering to each other like best friends. I raised my eyebrows as Bru got out of the jeep and turned on his charm to greet them.

"So, whose brilliant idea was *this*?" he asked, stepping up to the two of them.

"Pardon me?" asked the taller one. I could see in the hotel lights she was the older of the two.

Bru put an arm out and gestured at the dark. "Not a lot to see out there until that sun comes up. You do realize that, right?"

"Of course I do," she answered. "We want to watch the sunrise *from* the vortex so the whole thing will be that much more amazing." She stepped toward Bru and extended her hand. "I'm Julia Whitmore. You make this a transcendent experience for my daughter and me, and I'll make sure you're compensated for the early hour. You do realize *that*, right?"

She delivered her point with a wide smile, which Bru took to.

"Transcendent it is, then." He shook her hand. "I'm Bru. Climb in, and I'll get your gear."

Once they were loaded and settled into the back of the jeep and belted in, Bru turned the key and wiped the dusty rear-view mirror that spanned the whole top edge of the windshield. "Ladies, let me introduce a fellow traveler and seeker to you. This"—he gestured at me in the passenger seat—"is Honor. She's here on a spiritual journey too."

I looked at Bru, who just nodded at me, then I turned around to face them. "Hi. Nice to meet you."

"Honor? What a pretty name! Like, so . . . important sounding, you know? I'm Ashley. And this is my mom, Julia. We just got here two days ago."

Bru put the jeep in gear, and we rolled out of the turn-around and up a steep hill to the empty main road. "You ladies are gonna wanna finish that coffee of yours off before we hit the dirt," Bru called over his shoulder. "'Cuz as soon as we do, you're gonna get bumped around like you were in a stagecoach."

In the mirror, I watched them bring their cups to their lips almost in unison and sip silently, exchanging a glance, so I sipped too and watched the center line of the road in our headlights. We drove through the sleeping town in semiawkward silence, which wasn't all that surprising, considering it wasn't even five yet. Still, it seemed like someone should talk, so I turned around in my seat and looked at Ashley.

"So, where y'all visiting from?"

"California," she chirped. "Newport Beach." I felt Bru's

eyes on me in the mirror, but I didn't turn around. "What about you?" Ashley asked.

"Texas—no town you would've heard of, though."

"Funny thing, you being from California and all," Bru cut in. "That's where Honor here was headed before her car broke down." I looked over at him now, wondering why in the world he would feel the need to tell them this.

Julia laughed. "Really? It's not where I'd go on a spiritual journey. Maybe your car breaking down was the universe pointing you here instead."

I smiled politely. "Maybe so." She and Celia could have a field day with that one.

"Ohmygosh, it probably totally was!" Ashley's voice lit up, and she leaned forward and put her hand on my shoulder with the familiarity of an old friend. "We went to this psychic lady yesterday, and she told us all about how if your channels or chakras or something are all open and lined up, you can actually get messages from the universe about what it wants you to do." She paused for a quick breath before going on. *"And,"* she said, putting her other hand on Bru's shoulder, "she also said that this guy is the best guide in Sedona to take you to the vortex to hear it. The universe, I mean. So either you're lucky or it's meant to be!"

"Whew, girl," Bru said. "You talk like you've been here your whole life." He slowed the jeep and veered off onto a tree-lined dirt road. "I can't promise the universe is gonna tell you what to do with your life up there. But if you can keep quiet and listen close enough, for long enough, it may whisper something you need to hear." Bru winked at me. "Now hang on. It's about to get rough."

He shifted the jeep into a lower gear, and almost immediately the road stood up steep and rutted in front of us. We bounced hard over a big rock in the middle of it, and Ashley and Julia got quiet while Bru concentrated on navigating the so-called road. My eyes took in the silhouettes of trees and shrubs close by, and towering formations of rock all around us in every direction. The sun had yet to wash color into them, but already I was impressed by their sheer size. Nothing was this tall or majestic where I came from.

"Now, the vortex we're headed to this morning, ladies, is called an upflow vortex, meaning it's a place where energy flows *out* of the earth," Bru said over his shoulder. Julia and Ashley leaned forward to listen better, and he raised his voice. "The Native Americans used to come to this kind of vortex when they needed to commune with the Great Spirit, or like Ashley called it, the universe. They believed the energy flowing out of the earth carried their thoughts and questions up to the Great Spirit, and in return it gave them clarity and perspective."

"We all could use a little of that these days," Julia said from the back seat.

"True," Bru agreed. "But they were old hands at the art of meditation. Most of us these days aren't so good at that. We got too many other things going on, too much noise to listen to. Which is why my favorite thing to do is show people this place for the first time."

He took his foot off the gas and let the jeep coast to a stop, then pointed up the canyon to a massive rock silhouetted against the indigo sky. "That's it right there. Carousel Rock. You'll be a full mile above the valley up there. Enough to give anybody some perspective." He eased on the gas again, and we went back to bumping up the road.

"So, what do we do when we get up there?" Ashley asked. "Do you, like, chant or burn incense or something?"

I'd kind of been wondering the same thing. Wouldn't have been surprised if he'd said yes.

"Nope. When we get up there, that's when I'm gonna leave you ladies to yourselves. You split up—find your own little spot that draws you on the rock and go sit."

"And then?" Julia questioned.

Bru turned the wheel and shrugged. "And then see what happens. Close your eyes or keep 'em open. Whatever you feel like doing. And then just be still. And listen." He looked at Ashley in the rearview mirror. "Think you can do that, missy?"

Ashley sat up straight and serious. "Oh, yeah. Totally. I've been doing yoga for, like, two months."

"Good." He nodded. "Honor?"

"Yep. Helps I didn't get much sleep last night. I don't feel like doing much else."

"All right then," Bru said. We were quiet as we climbed up the canyon to Carousel Rock, maybe pondering what the universe would have to say to us.

19

"Um, Bru? Is there a place to pee before I go listen to the universe?" Ashley was hopping from one foot to the other while her mom climbed out of the jeep.

"Yep—we got boy trees and girl trees out here." He pointed across the dirt road at a hillside dotted with cactus and sage brush. "Just don't get too friendly with the spiky ones. I'll wait right here for ya."

"I'll go with you, honey," Julia said, and she and Ashley linked arms to go find a couple of girl trees. I got out of the jeep and stretched in the cool morning air.

"You wanna head up first, go right ahead," Bru said. He pointed to a narrow trail that snaked up the base of the rock. "Just watch your step. And once you're up there, find your place and sit awhile." He turned around and checked the ridge behind him, where the deep blue was already fading to light. "Sun should be up in twenty minutes or so."

"Okay," I answered, still not sure how this was all supposed to go, really. But it felt good to be up and out in the mountain-fresh air, seeing the sunrise for the second day in a row.

I gave Bru a nod, then set off up the rocky trail, wondering for the hundredth time in the last few days what in the world I was doing. While the rest of the freshmen at ATU were touring campus and bonding with their roommates, I was walking up a mountain, holding out a tiny hope for some answers.

In the weak light it was pretty easy to make my way up the trail and over the base of the red rock that jutted up to the sky. When I got to a point where I had to climb, I wedged my boot in a wide crack and my fingers in another. I pulled myself up onto my knees, right beside a gnarled juniper tree that twisted its way out of the deep red of the rock. Then I breathed in deep and sat down right there, because I knew. If there was any place that felt like I was meant to be, it was this one.

I scanned the sky, hoping to catch another glimpse of a shooting star, but it was already too light. Immediately below me was the wide canyon we'd driven up, the road cutting a thin beige line through the thick blanket of green pines. But between the town and the canyon lay the most stunningly beautiful part of the whole scene. Towers and peaks and mountains of rock, all jagged and weather worn, rose out of the thin mist that covered the valley. They stood wise and silent, layer upon layer of color and time, stacked tall enough to kiss the stars. I'd never seen time stretch back so far like that, and all at once I felt smaller than I ever had. Like a pinprick of light in an infinite purple sky.

Finn would've said that was exactly right. That's what we are. His particular brand of spirituality was always wrapped up in that sky. When our parents died, he didn't go to church for comfort or answers. He went to the roof instead. And he took me with him. The first time I saw him climbing out his bedroom window I burst into panicked tears, thinking he was running away, leaving me all alone. Minutes later, when we lay there on the roof with a blanket of stars spread over us and our backs pressed into the still-warm shingles, he promised he would never leave me.

And yet here I was. Alone. I didn't want to be angry with him for that, wanted more than anything to understand, so I closed my eyes against the sky to listen for some little bit of truth or peace. Anything the universe was willing to give. A breeze drifted soft and cool over my face. In the distance, I thought I heard the cry of a hawk. Then I heard something closer. A voice.

"Honor!" It whispered excitedly. "I hope you believe in fate. Because Kyra Kelley is my *cousin*."

I whipped around to see Ashley behind me, trying desperately to hoist herself up to where I sat. "*What?* What are you talking about?" I hadn't heard her coming at all.

She stuck her tiny hand out to me. "Pull me up! This is crazy!"

I leaned over and grabbed her hand with both of mine, then dug my heels in and pulled while she pushed, until she popped up onto the rock next to me. She didn't waste a second. "Okay, I have to say this quick because we're supposed to be meditating and all, *but*—Bru told me all about the letter and the tickets your brother sent you and your journey to go see Kyra's last show and everything, and I just know this was meant to be. You *have* to make it there. It's, like, a pilgrimage or something."

She paused, the most excited smile on her face, waiting for me to answer, but I didn't know where to even begin. Ashley took that as a cue to keep going.

"Okay, so here's the plan—I'll call her and tell her your whole story and let her know you're coming to the show, and then I'll give you her assistant's number to call when you get there. She can meet you and take you backstage after, which will be amazing, since it's her last show ever, and then—"

"Wait a sec." I grabbed one of her hands, hoping it might help her stop talking for a minute. "Why did Bru tell you all that? It wasn't any of his business—"

"I asked him," Ashley said simply. "Because you seemed so sad. And so he told me. Which couldn't be more perfect, and *definitely* isn't coincidence." She pointed up at the sky and brought her voice back down to a whisper. "It's the universe. And it's saying you're on the right path."

I stared at her in the faint morning light, smiling hope right at me as the sun rose golden warm behind the ridge, and I believed her. For some reason I didn't yet know or understand, I was really supposed to make it to Kyra Kelley. And this random girl was holding the door wide open for me. "You think she'll *actually* see me? In person?" I managed.

Ashley nodded emphatically. "Yes! I can't wait to tell her about this. She's *totally* into this kind of stuff right now."

Despite what I'd said to Rusty about not being that excited to see Kyra Kelley anymore, the thought of actually meeting her brought back my little fangirl urge to jump up and down and squeal about it. Instead, I grabbed Ashley's dainty, perfectly manicured hands and said, "Thank you. You have no idea what this means to me. Really. It's . . ."

"It's what I do." Ashley smiled. She gazed thoughtfully out over the valley. "I'm actually kind of good at it—helping people, I mean."

I leaned my back against the tree and watched as a hot-air balloon rose in slow motion from the valley floor. "Maybe that's the universe telling *you* something."

"Maybe so." She patted my knee. "I'm gonna go sit and see if it says anything else before Bru or my mom comes up here and tells me I need to be quiet."

I gave her my hand so she could lower herself down the rock, which she did quite gracefully. Once down, she turned to walk away but then paused and looked back up at me. "I'm really sorry about your brother, Honor."

"Thank you."

"And . . . for what it's worth . . . I bet good things will happen for you. That's how it should work, anyway."

She turned again, and I watched as she picked her way gingerly down the trail, then disappeared over a little ridge. The sun fell warm on my back and splashed color into the rocks all around so that they bloomed soft and hopeful in the light of a new day. And as I sat there watching, something in me did too.

20

By the time Bru and I rumbled up the dirt driveway to his house, the heat of the day was coming on fast. We'd dropped off Ashley and her mom, washed down the jeep, and gone to breakfast, all before ten o'clock. And now I was anxious to get the Pala fixed up and keep going, all the way to California and Kyra Kelley. Which was a real possibility, thanks to Ashley and the little piece of fate folded up in my pocket. She'd written Kyra's assistant's cell number on a stray receipt and assured me she'd be expecting to hear from me soon. I couldn't wait to tell Celia I thought she was right and show Rusty that maybe I wasn't crazy after all.

When we came to a stop, I glimpsed him sitting on an overturned bucket next to the Pala's open hood, beer in hand, and my mood took a nosedive. Ah. It would be that kind of Rusty today. I took my time getting out of the jeep when Bru turned it off, thanked him again for taking me along, then walked begrudgingly over to Rusty.

"Well, don't you look all refreshed and enlightened this morning," he said with the exact flat kind of sarcasm I'd been expecting.

"Probably better off than you." I eyed his beer. "Isn't it a little early for that?"

He glanced up at me, then took a long drink from the bottle. "Prerequisite for working on cars. Right, Bru?"

"Whatever gets you goin', I guess." Bru waved his hands in an I'm-not-getting-into-this surrender as he walked by and went into the house.

I waited for the door to shut behind him before I turned back to Rusty, all sass and smugness. "Doesn't look like you're working very hard."

"That's 'cuz I'm done." He set the bottle in the dirt and stood as I walked over to the car. "I got good news and bad news."

"What's the good?" I asked, hoping it was that he'd gotten it fixed already, so we could get back on the road as soon as possible.

Rusty stepped over to the open hood of the Pala and surveyed the inside. "Good news is that the radiator's fine. It's a connector hose that has a leak, and that's a cheaper fix."

"Okay," I said cautiously. "What's the bad news, then?"

"Bad news is that shops don't stock parts for fifty-year-old cars."

No, no, no. This couldn't happen, not now. Panic leaped into my throat. "The concert's the day after tomorrow. We have to get there. Can't we rush-order one or something?"

"Did that already," he said, leaning on the car. "There's a guy in Fresno that Finn and I got a bunch of parts from when we were first fixin' her up. I gave him a call, and he said he'd send a hose that should fit, but it'll be a day before it gets here."

"A day, as in *tomorrow*? And then you can fix it and we can go?" I started running through back-up plans in my mind before Rusty could answer. Maybe I could rent a car for the rest of the way.

"How much is it gonna cost?" I asked him. I hadn't figured on having to fix the car. Actually, I hadn't really *figured* anything for this trip. I'd had Finn's ATM card, which I sometimes used if Gina was running low or if there was something special I wanted. But I had no idea how much money was in the account, and now seemed like a good time to start worrying about it.

"I got it," Rusty answered.

"No, this is my mess. And now my car. You don't have to pay for that. I just need to know how much it's going to cost."

Rusty sighed, exasperated. "I said I got it, okay?" He turned and shut the hood gently, giving it a pat. "It's been a while since I bought Pala anything nice. She's been neglected lately."

I almost rolled my eyes but stopped short. I'd take this kind of chivalry, even if it was meant for the car. "Well, thanks. That's . . . that's nice of you." I looked at the ground and outlined a circle in the red dust with the toe of my boot, not sure what to say after that.

Rusty pushed off the car and turned on his heels to face me. "Don't thank me yet. I don't know how far she'll make it even after we get it fixed. Lots of times, one problem like this leads to a whole bunch of other ones real quick. Just makin' it there may be shaky, let alone back home."

I thought of the car breaking down and us ending up here, and meeting Ashley, and my ticket to meet Kyra Kelley tucked safely in my pocket, and I hoped with everything in me that we'd make it to her, because now I knew we were supposed to.

"I bet it'll be okay," I said. "We'll just have to go easy."

Rusty didn't seem convinced. "We'll see." He bent down and grabbed his half-full beer, then walked it over to the trash can in the carport. "We got at least a day to kill anyway," he said, coming back. "We can drive my mom's truck until then if there's someplace you wanna go."

"Like where?"

"I don't know. There's plenty of places. It's better than sittin' around here all day while Bru takes a nap and my mom goes on about how psychic she is."

I thought about it. "How 'bout NAU? You can show me the stadium where you play."

He shook his head. "Nah, I don't feel like going up there today."

There was something in his voice, but I didn't push it. "All right. What about somewhere you *do* wanna go? I don't know what's around. You're the one who's been going to school up here. Surprise me." I hoped he'd take it as a peace offering after last night.

Rusty mulled it over a minute and I waited, feeling the sun sink into me.

"I got a couple places," he said finally. "Grab your bathing suit. And something to throw on after."

21

Turned out driving around in Celia's truck wasn't all that different from driving around in the Pala. It had to be just as old, with its rounded red fenders and cab and dusty smell. And the lack of AC. We drove with the windows down, the radio up, and one arm each resting on the doors. Hot wind rushed through the cab, blowing my hair loose and wild, and it felt like freedom heading down the highway like that. Out my window, great peaks of rock, all sundrenched and windswept, rose in odd formations against an impossibly blue sky. On Rusty's side, the rocks gave way to wide open country that ended at the horizon, where the sky met the red-orange earth like a giant dome pinned tight to the edges.

We sat across from each other on the bench seat, easy and relaxed in the way that reminded me of the long days of summer when you have nothing but time on your hands. I decided to try and keep it that way, because I wanted to hold on to the hopeful feeling I'd had at the vortex. It seemed like he had decided to do the same, because he didn't mention anything about the previous night either, and we drove on in Celia's old Chevy truck, with its radio that only picked up one country station, which was just fine with me.

"So, where're we going?" I yelled over the wind and twangy guitar.

"Thought you wanted me to surprise you," Rusty answered, just as loud.

I turned the radio down. "And when you tell me, I'll be surprised."

He didn't answer. Just kept his eyes on the road and chewed his gum slowly, long enough to make me wonder if he'd heard me. "Swimmin'," he said finally.

"Yeah, I got that part." I snapped my bathing suit strap. "Just wondering where, is all."

"Here," Rusty said, slowing the truck. He turned us off the highway onto a narrow road marked CRESCENT MOON RANCH. We drove through a little kiosk with nobody in it to take any money, and continued down the road to a parking lot, where a few dusty cars were scattered. We parked off on our own and stepped out into the waves of heat rising off the asphalt. Rusty walked around to the back of the truck, but I stood a minute, taking in the view. Across a wide, grassy field, trees crowded together thick and green, in a meandering line I knew meant there was a creek. Maybe like the one we'd played in on summer days as kids. Beyond that was another mountain of rock so red it didn't look like it could be real. I walked back to where Rusty was leaned into the truck bed, reaching for something. "How'd you know about this place? It's so pretty."

He grabbed a little cooler and a couple of towels. "A chick from school brought me down here once." He smiled slow and to himself, and I knew there must be a story behind that one, but I didn't need to hear it, so I didn't bother asking what her name was.

I motioned at the cooler. "Any food in there, or is it just full of beer?"

"Lunch," he answered, tucking the towels under one arm. Then he shook his head. "My mom sent it. Which means it probably ain't edible."

I laughed. "That was nice of her, anyhow."

"Yep. You ready?" He stood there waiting for me to answer, looking almost sweet, if I didn't know him so well. It set off a little ripple in my stomach that ended in a smile I tried to hide by looking away.

"Yeah, let's go," I said. "I need to cool off."

The narrow dirt trail led us right down into the shade of the trees, where it was damp and fresh smelling, and cooler right away. I followed behind Rusty and every few seconds caught a glimpse of water sparkling out in the open, beneath the sun. Blackberry bushes spread out tangly and wild along our path, throwing splashes of deep purple into the green all around. And a little stream, deep with cool water, snaked its way alongside the trail, gurgling over rocks as it went.

"Almost there," Rusty said over his shoulder. "Hopefully we'll have it to ourselves."

The stream widened as we walked a few more quiet steps,

and Rusty stopped at a bridge of rocks someone had built across it. He hopped on the middle one, then to the other side, and waited for me to do the same before continuing down the path that I could see led down to a wide, lazy part of the main creek. Once I caught up to him, we took the last few steps together until we were standing at the edge of the perfect swimming hole.

The borders of the creek were shaded by hanging branches of trees, but in the middle, the sun shone right down into deep, blue-green water. An image of him and his 'chick from school' tangled together, laughing in the water, flashed in my mind for a second and I shook it away quick. Still. I couldn't blame her, whoever she'd been. If he were a guy I liked and I was as brave as I wished I was, that's what I might bring him here to do. . . . I pushed that thought from my head just as fast. What was wrong with me?

Rusty turned to me. "You good with hanging out here awhile?"

"You're kidding, right? I could stay here for days."

I looked across the creek to where the rocks rose a good fifteen feet above the water, and my eyes found the best part of the whole place. Strung from the branch of a leaning tree, long enough to take you sailing right out into the deepest part of the water, was a rope swing. I wondered for a second if his choice of spot had anything to do with what I'd said in the car about his and Finn's old rope swing. Like maybe this was a small, sweet gesture on his part. Either way, it was the perfect place to waste a day away.

Rusty motioned up at them and the swing. "You feelin' brave today, H?"

"You mean the swing? It's not *that* high." I gave it another look. "People go off it, don't they?"

"Sure." He shrugged. "Just looks a helluva lot higher from the top, is all." He threw me one of those smiles of his that I knew was actually a challenge.

I smiled it right back at him. "Let's go."

"You sure? It's pretty damn high. . . ."

"I think I can handle it. I'm all grown up now, remember?" *Oh my god, I did not just say that.*

I walked over to a little area of smooth red rock that sloped gently down into the creek, kicked off my sandals, and shook my hair out behind me. Then, just like I'd done the day before, only a little slower and a lot more to the point, I slid my shorts down my legs and pulled my tank top over my head. At least I was in an actual bikini this time. A cute little black one with pink trim that I was kinda proud to show off.

Rusty shook his head, his smile turning into a laugh.

"What?" I asked, immediately on alert. Was I untied? Showing something I shouldn't be? *What?*

"Nothin'," he said, crossing his arms. Then he shook his head again. "I just keep forgetting."

"Forgetting *what*?" I asked. My attempt at sassiness was crumbling into self-consciousness by the second, but I did my best to hang on to it. Or come up with something else to say that didn't sound like such a lame come-on.

His eyes ran over me quick then leaped out to the water. "That you're all grown up," he said. "Guess I just keep forgetting."

I didn't know whether to be happy I'd reminded him or mad he kept forgetting, but we'd be coming up on an awfully awkward moment if I just stood there any longer. I motioned at the water. "You getting in, or am I going alone?"

Rusty raised an eyebrow, then kicked his sandals off and pulled his T-shirt over his head, revealing the same broad shoulders that had so impressed me the day before. I hadn't forgotten about those and how grown up *he* seemed. "After you," he said like a gentleman, sweeping a tan arm out toward the water.

I held his eyes for just a second. Long enough, I hoped, to say something. No matter that I didn't know what. Then I took a two-step running start off the edge of the creek and dove right into the middle of it, through the sun-warmed surface, and down into the cool quiet of its deepest part, where water flowed silently over rock like it probably had for years and years.

I heard Rusty splash into the water next to me, felt the bubbles rush by and then the brush of his skin across my legs, just quick enough to send sparks right up them. I came up first, my breath stolen a bit by the coolness of the water or the warmth of his skin, or both. Rusty popped up right next to me, close, and we treaded water for a few seconds without saying anything.

"So," he asked finally. "You wanna try it out?"

I blinked water out of my eyes. "Yeah. Sure." It sounded way more sure than I actually was. "It does look a little taller from down here, though. How high *is* it?"

"I don't know," Rusty said, swimming by me. "Maybe twenty feet . . . twenty-five. You'll be fine. C'mon." In about four strokes, he was on the other side of the creek, pulling himself up the steep side of the rock. I hesitated a second before following him, not entirely sure this was something I wanted to do but feeling like I might've gotten myself in too far to back out now. When I got to the edge, Rusty reached a hand down and pulled me up to my feet all in one motion, like it was nothing.

"We go up right here." He pointed at another rope strung down the side of the rock. It was knotted every couple of feet so that you could hold on to it while you climbed up the faint footholds worn into the side. Rusty led the way up, grabbing each knot and using it to pull himself up. I did the same, but with a growing feeling of dread every few feet. When I finally pulled myself up that last step, to the top of the rock, a cloud of butterflies took flight in my stomach, swirling around each other in a wild swarm.

We were high. Nauseatingly high. Way higher than it'd looked from the other side of the creek. High enough to make me wish I'd never opened my mouth about it, because I was not about to throw myself off this rock to prove anything to anybody. Even if he was all dripping wet and tan and strong.

Rusty grabbed a stick, then walked over to the edge of the rock and hooked the rope with it. Once he had the rope, he looked up and gave it a few good, firm tugs before turning to me with a smile the size of Texas. Like he knew I was having a heart attack about this. "It's good to go."

I swallowed and straightened up my shoulders. "Okay. Are you sure?"

"Yep. This thing's been here forever."

Great. "Okay," I answered, my voice a notch or two higher than normal. I tried not to be too obvious about the deep breath I attempted to take. "Okay," I said again—more for myself than anything else. I walked over to the rope and gave it a tug, then peered down into the center of the water, which now looked even farther away. *Breathe.*

"You want me to go first?" Rusty asked.

"No, no. I can do it. Just . . . working up my courage." I did my best at a smile.

Rusty stepped up next to me and grabbed the rope. "Just get your hands up here and get a good grip, then take a running start when you jump. It's gonna swoop you down at first and then arc you up over the middle of the creek. When you feel yourself go up like that, let go."

"Okay," I said for the fiftieth time. *Breathe.* It was time to just go and do it, just take those couple of steps off the edge and do it. I tightened up my grip on the rope and backed up. Rusty stepped aside, arms crossed over his chest, and nodded encouragement at me like a coach or something. I took one more breath. I wanted to be fearless, I did. Finn had been. And Rusty, he was always the kind of reckless you either admired or shook your head at. I, on the other hand, didn't want to die jumping off this rock today, even if it meant losing a little dignity.

"Nope," I said, letting the rope drop. "I can't do it." I backed up, disappointed in myself, and waited for the inevitable teasing to follow.

"You sure?" Rusty asked.

"Yep. And you don't have to tell me what a chicken I am. I know, okay?" I crossed my arms over my chest, already planning my route down.

Rusty shrugged. "Doesn't matter to me if you jump." He

grabbed the rope swinging between us. "I woulda been surprised if you did. Takes some balls."

"Let's see yours then," I said, irritated he'd thought I wouldn't do it.

"My balls?" Rusty laughed.

Why did I never think before I said something like that? "That's not what I meant, you perve. Your jump. If you didn't think I was gonna jump, that must be what we're up here to see." I stepped to the side all huffy, clearing him a path. "So go. Impress me."

Rusty smirked and took a step back. "Now, why would I need to do that?"

I opened my mouth to respond, then decided to do that thing where you think before you speak. "Never mind. Do what you want. I'm going back down to swim." I turned without waiting for him to answer and lowered myself down to the first foothold, intent on acting as uninterested as I could.

"Suit yourself," he called after me.

I could hear the smile in his voice, and I knew he was gonna jump. When I got to the bottom, I sat down on the rock at the edge of the creek, dipped my feet in, and waited. Sure enough, about two seconds later, Rusty let out a yell and came sailing over the edge of the rock, all momentum and force. He flew down, fast and far in a wide arc, and when he got to the top of it, in that tiny moment between up and down, he didn't just let go. He threw his body backward into a flip that came all the way around just before he plunged into the water, sending up a splash that reached me even at the edge.

It took a few seconds for him to come up, but when he

did, he shook his hair out, clearly proud of himself, and he looked over at me, bright eyed and a little out of breath.

"Show-off," I said, trying not to smile.

He swam over to where I sat and dipped his chin in the water, then spit a fountainlike stream up in the air. "Thought you were gonna swim."

I leaned back on my elbows. "I am, in a little while."

"No you're not," he said, inching closer.

"I *am*. Leave me alone about it." I splashed him with my foot.

He shook his head with a smile. "No. You're gonna swim right now." I knew an instant before he did it what was about to happen, but I didn't have any time to defend myself. He grabbed the rock and pulled himself out of the water just enough to wrap his arms around me and take me back in with him. I screamed just before we went under together and twisted around enough to get free and to the surface.

When he came up, I cut my hand into the water and splashed at him, then turned and took off as fast as I could without waiting to see if he'd chase me. I knew he would. He caught me quick, probably in two strokes, and I dug in harder to escape before he dunked me again, but it was no use. I was laughing, and he was too, and there we were, tangled up together in the water and sunshine. In a good kind of way.

22

The branches hanging above me cut the cobalt sky into puzzle pieces that shifted and changed ever so slightly in the breeze. I watched them quietly, not sure if Rusty was still even awake. After dunking each other multiple times, we'd swum and laughed and floated around before pulling ourselves slowly from the water. And now we lay stretched out on the sun-drenched rock at the edge of the creek, almost close enough to touch, but miles away from it at the same time.

I closed my eyes and listened to the occasional chirps of tiny birds hidden in the trees around us, the bubbling of water over rocks down below, cicadas rattling a chorus off in the distance. All sounds of the world carrying on like it always had. So much could change or be lost, and still, the rest of the world went on like it was nothing. It didn't seem wrong, but it didn't seem right either. *I'd* gone on today like it was nothing. I'd laughed and felt happy and forgotten for a little while that this was now a world without my brother in it.

But Finn wouldn't ever get to drive in the Pala again or jump off a crazy swing with Rusty or watch the clouds drift by on a lazy summer day. He wouldn't get to go to college and play football with his best friend or meet someone perfect, fall in love, and get married. He wouldn't be there to give me away when I did. He'd given it all up, changed all the plans, and that was what seemed the most wrong. Because he didn't have to, and nobody wanted him to, but he did. I squeezed my eyes tight and tried to breathe away the guilt that had shifted ever so slightly into anger at the unfairness of it.

"You all right?" Rusty's hand on my shoulder surprised me more than his voice did.

I sat up, wiping at my eyes. "I'm fine. I just . . ."

"It kinda comes and goes, huh?" He looked out over the water, then back to me, and I wished he couldn't see so much just then.

I put my head down. "Yeah."

"I know," Rusty said. He put his arm around my shoulder. "It does with me, too." A soft breeze rose and swirled around us, and off in the distance, a muffled rumble of thunder seemed to answer.

"Must be four o'clock," Rusty said, eyeing the fluffy gray clouds that had rolled in over the mountaintops. Lightning flickered behind one, and its thunder came a few seconds later.

"What does that mean?" I asked, wiping my eyes.

"Means we better head out. Before we get soaked."

He had no sooner finished saying it than the first fat drop splashed down on the rock between us. I looked at the spot where it landed, and another one plopped right down on my head.

"Too late." I smiled. I reached for my clothes, and Rusty did the same, and by the time we crossed the little bridge, raindrops had splattered our rock a deeper shade of red and turned the smooth surface of the creek into a collage of expanding rings. When we hit the green twisting path, thunder boomed loud above us and the sky opened up, sending fat raindrops down through the trees, and we ran.

We ran laughing, with the smell of the rain all around and the drops cool on our skin, across the grassy field to the parking lot, where Celia's old truck sat all alone. I threw open the door on my side and jumped in, shutting it hard behind me. Rusty ducked into the driver's side and shook his hair out before he closed the door.

"So much for not getting soaked," I said, out of breath. I ran my hands down my bare arms, then shook the water off. "That came out of nowhere."

"They roll in pretty quick around here." Rusty's eyes ran over my wet clothes. "You got something dry to put on?"

"Yeah. It's down there." I motioned to the floor, where a sundress sat draped over my boots. "I'll be fine till we get back to your mom's, though. I don't need to change right now."

He turned the key in the ignition. "I don't wanna go back there just yet. It'd be a long night of sittin' around doin' nothing." He thought for a second. "There's a place up in Flagstaff, has good music and the best burger you ever tasted. You hungry?"

"Yes." I definitely was. Celia's "lunch" had consisted of two seaweed and alfalfa sandwiches on sprouted wheat bread, a concoction that was good for cleansing and grounding. That's what the note said, anyway. "I can always eat." I smiled. I didn't want to go back just yet either.

"Yes you can," Rusty said with a smile. "It's one of your better qualities." He put his arm on the seat behind me and twisted around to back the truck out. "That and your little black bikini."

"Shut up," I said, trying not to smile too big. "Just drive. I'm starving."

23

By the time we got to Flagstaff, the rain had stopped, but the afternoon clouds still lit up every few seconds as the storm rolled off into the distance. We turned off the highway at a huge guitar balanced on a marquee shaped like one of those old-fashioned Route 66 road signs. Across it, in big black letters, it said, WADE BOWEN HERE TONIGHT!

"I know him!" I said, pointing at the sign as we pulled into the parking lot. "Well, I don't *know* him know him, but I know his music."

"He's a Texas boy. New Braunfels, I think," Rusty said. "Pretty good, too." He parked Celia's truck around the side of the log cabin–looking building. "Depending on who's working, we might be able to stay for the show."

"Really?"

"We'll see." Rusty reached behind his seat and pulled out

jeans, a T-shirt, and his boots. "C'mon. Let's go get changed and get some grub."

Inside, it was dark and so full of things to look at, I didn't know where to start. It was definitely a down-home, Rusty kind of place, with its antlers and stuffed animal heads of all different sizes on the wall. Autographed pictures of country singers and old-time cowboys hung everywhere, lit by the glow of scattered neon beer signs. Past the tables in front was a giant wooden bar, where three old cowboys sat talking with beers and a basket of peanuts between them. I liked it right off the bat.

Rusty pointed me to the girls' bathroom and then ducked into the one across the hall, and when we both came out, he headed over to one of the round booths at the edge of the room.

I scooted across the red leather, to the back of it. "This place is great. How'd you find it?"

"That big sign out there." I gave him a look. "What? It was advertising DIME BEER NIGHT, and I came on in."

"They serve you beer here? You have an ID?"

"Something like that," Rusty said with a smirk.

Before I could ask him anything else, a waitress dressed in tight jeans and an even tighter tank top slid up to the table. Her name tag said SHANA. "Hey, stranger," she drawled at Rusty. "Where you been?" She looked like she was about to sit in his lap. And I bet he would've liked it too. She was just the way he probably liked a girl to look: long dark hair, heavy-lined eyes, shiny lips, and boobs about to burst right out of her top. I decided I didn't like her.

"Went back home for a little while," Rusty said, clearing his throat.

Shana looked pained all of a sudden. "Oh my gosh, I'm so sorry. J.D. mentioned something about that. We were all awfully sorry to hear about your friend. That was the same guy who came up here with you on a trip to check out the team a few years back, right?"

"Shana, this is Honor," Rusty interrupted. "His sister."

"Oh," she said, turning to me. "I'm so sorry. About your brother. It must be really hard for you."

I just nodded, hoping she'd get the drift that it wasn't something I wanted to talk about at the moment. Half of me felt guilty for the thought, but the other half just wanted a little stretch of time where it didn't weigh so heavy on me.

Shana spoke up. "My fiancé was the captain who took him all around, so I met him when he was up here. Good guy."

Fiancé. I nodded again. Maybe she wasn't so bad.

"Kinda like Rusty here." She patted him firmly on the shoulder.

He raised his eyebrows and opened up his menu. "I don't know if I'd go that far."

"I definitely wouldn't," I added, relieved for a change in subject.

"Oh, then you haven't seen this boy dance." Shana smiled. "Not many players are as good on the dance floor as they are on the field. Believe me, I've dated my fair share of 'em." She said this behind her hand, like she was telling me a secret. Rusty nodded agreement from behind his menu. "But Rusty here," Shana continued, "can make anyone look good on the dance floor." I watched him smile behind his menu and tried to picture it. "You guys should stay for Wade Bowen tonight," she offered. "Then you can see for yourself."

I was liking this girl more and more. "That sounds good, thank you." I kicked Rusty under the table. "We're stayin', right?"

"Fine with me." He closed his menu and smiled up at Shana. "I'll take one of those western burgers and a Bud, if it's not too much trouble."

"It's not at all," she said without writing it down. "What about you, Honor? What can I getcha?"

"I'll take the same," I said, more joking than anything.

"Sure thing. I'll put those in right now and be back with your beers." Shana winked and turned on the heel of her boot.

When she was gone, Rusty raised an eyebrow at me from across the table. "Gutsy."

"What?" I asked like it was nothing. "You ordered one no problem." I tried not to smile but couldn't contain the pride I felt at having just ordered a beer. In a restaurant. From a waitress.

"That's right. I forgot," Rusty said with a slow smile. "You're all grown up these days."

Shana returned with two frosty beer bottles and set them on the table in front of us. "Burgers'll be up in a few. You guys need anything else?"

"Actually, I think we do." Rusty sat back against the booth and looked up at her with the kind of smile that could probably make most girls say yes to anything. "We were thinkin' we might need a couple of shots to go along with these."

Shana tilted her head at him like the answer was no. "What

about Hell Week? You guys aren't supposed to be drinkin' heavy right now."

"It's to toast to her brother." He motioned at me, then looked back up at her, very serious. It was shameless, but something Finn probably would have appreciated. "C'mon. For Honor."

Shana glanced at me, mulling it over before she turned back to Rusty. "Fine. Just don't tell coach it was me that knocked you off the wagon. And keep it low key. I can't afford to get in trouble over you, okay?"

We both nodded.

"What do you want, then?"

Rusty gave the question over to me. "Honor? What're we drinkin'?"

Another one of his dares. I should've never, ever said anything about being all grown up. It was the exact type of thing he wouldn't let me live down. Fine then. I pretended to think about it, like I actually knew something about what I might like to drink. "Hmm . . ."

Rusty watched me, entertained, and Shana waited.

"Tequila," I said finally, with conviction. No matter that I'd never actually drunk tequila. It was the first booze that popped into my head, mostly because I'd heard enough songs to know it was something people took shots of.

Shana arched an eyebrow at Rusty, and he shrugged. "The girl means business. Make it two. And a couple more Buds to go with."

"Oh good lord," Shana said, shaking her head. "I can already see what kind of night this one's gonna be. I'll be right back."

She turned again and headed for the bar, and I watched the

cowboys watch her hips sway as she walked by. Then something she'd said came back to me. "You're s'posed to be in Hell Week right now?" Rusty rubbed his forehead but didn't answer. "Are you?"

"I guess so." He lifted his beer and took a long drink, then set it down in a way that said he was done with that question. He wasn't playing anymore, then. Shana just didn't know it yet. "So, Honor, tell me somethin'. You a big tequila fan these days?"

"Oh come on. I had to order something. You used Finn to call me out on that." Really, I'd regretted it as soon as I'd said it. The only hard alcohol I'd ever drunk was some peach schnapps that Lilah got once, and that was pretty nasty. Other than that, it was a beer here and there, but not because it tasted good. That was just what you walked around a party with. I picked mine up and took a big gulp. Since we were in a bar and all.

"That's fine," Rusty said. "I just didn't know you could handle the hard stuff." He raised his bottle casually for another sip.

"I should be able to. Why wouldn't I? It can't be *that* bad, right?"

"Nah, it's not that bad." He sat back with a wide grin and watched Shana, who was weaving her way back to us, tray held high above her head.

When she got to the table, she took two more beers off the tray first, then set down in front of me what looked way bigger than I thought a shot glass should be. "It's a double," she said. "On the house."

This was gonna be bad. "Thank you." I smiled up at her,

trying not to look scared of it. I slid it closer to me, spilling some on my hand. Oh god. I could smell it from far away.

Rusty took his and turned to Shana with a smile as she set down a dish of limes. "Thank you, ma'am."

"Burgers'll be up soon, okay? Enjoy." She hustled off to tend to the bar, which was now filling up with cowboys, mostly older guys milling around in boots and palm-leaf hats.

Rusty looked at me like he was working hard to keep a straight face, then he licked the back of his hand and picked up the salt shaker.

"What are you doing?"

He sprinkled salt over the wet spot. "I'm takin' this shot. Salt?"

Apparently this was how you took a shot of tequila. With salt. I stuck my hand out.

He grinned. "Did you want me to lick it for you?"

"Ew. No." I pulled my hand back and licked it myself. "This is weird. Are you messin' with me?"

"No," he said, sprinkling salt on my hand. "You lick the salt, take the shot, then suck on one of these." He put a lime wedge between the thumb and forefinger of my salted hand, then slid the shot over to my free hand. "Pick your glass up now."

I did, and Rusty grabbed himself a lime, then raised his glass in his other hand. He actually expected me to do this. Right now. The smell of it was enough to make me wanna heave. My heart sped up. I was just gonna have to get it down as fast as I could without thinking about it. But oh, god, it was gonna be nasty.

"To Finn," Rusty said, clinking my glass.

"To Finn," I echoed. For a brief second I wondered what he'd think of this. Then I licked the salt off my hand, just like Rusty did, which was gross, but that was nothing compared to the nasty burn of the tequila I threw down my throat. Everything in me shivered and tried to gag it back up, but I forced it down, then jammed the lime in my mouth, hard.

"*Nicely* done," Rusty said from across the table. He licked his lips and went for his beer.

I kept the lime pressed to my teeth and breathed through my nose, willing the shot to stay in my stomach, where it now swam around all warm and tingly. When I was pretty sure it was gonna stay put, I took the lime out.

"That," I said, grabbing for my beer, "was horrible." I took a good, long gulp that washed away the last of the burn and gave me a new appreciation for beer, then I set the half-empty bottle on the table and shook my head at Rusty. "Ugh. No tequila. Ever again."

24

"YOU SHOULD TRY SOME MORE TEQUILA!" I yell across the table to Rusty. "IT'LL CHANGE YOUR LIFE!"

He laughs and says something I can't hear because the music is so loud. Who cares. Wade Bowen's up on the stage with his cute raspy twang and his guitar, and out on the dance floor everyone's spinning and girls are flying up in the air and I'm gonna go out there too. I belong out there.

I scooch around the curve of the booth to Rusty's side so he can hear me, then loop my arm through his and pull. "WE SHOULD DANCE! C'MON!" I twirl my finger around in the air. "BECAUSE *THIS* IS A REALLY GOOD SONG!"

Rusty leans away from me, laughing. "Goddamn, you're drunk. And loud. You should maybe test out standing up first." He nods at the couple, maybe three, empty rounds on the table.

"Whatever, I'm fine." I take my arm back. "You're no fun.

I'm gonna go get one of those cowboys to dance with." I go to scoot out of the booth for the guy I've been watching all night. He's tall and cute and does this little move where he flips his hat off his head whenever he spins a girl. I want him to spin me and flip his hat.

Rusty grabs my arm. "Lemme finish this beer. Then we'll dance."

"Promise? I don't believe you."

"I promise."

"Fine." I grab his beer out of his hand and take a drink, and he just shakes his head. "What? I'm helping you. So we can dance."

"Okay, have at it then."

I go for another drink, and it's kinda warm and not very good. But Rusty hits me with those green eyes of his and smiles, and *that* is very good. I wonder if he knows I just thought that. Oh crap, he does know. That's why he's still smiling. I should change the subject.

"I have a question for you," I say, very serious, like I've been thinking it over forever. Because I have, actually. "Why do you—and Finn did it too. . . . Why do you guys talk about the Pala like it's a girl? Why do guys *do* that with things? Do you know how dumb it sounds?"

Rusty just looks at me for a second, then cracks up. And then I do too, and I don't even know what's so funny except that he's laughing and trying to catch his breath and every time he's about to, it starts all over again.

"Really," I ask through tears. "Why do you *do* that?"

Rusty leans back and breathes in deep, still on the edge of laughing. "Oh, goddamn, that's funny."

"What?" I'm about to start up with the giggles again, and I still don't know what was funny in the first place.

"It's not 'the Pala,' it's Paula."

"Huh?"

"Finn's car. We named it after a girl—Paula."

"No. You're wrong." I poke him in the chest for emphasis. "Pala . . . is short for *Im*pala. Duh. Finn never knew anyone named Paula."

Rusty crumbles into a laugh again. "That's what you thought this whole time?"

"Yeah . . ." Is he . . . he's laughing at *me*.

"No . . ." He catches his breath again. "Paula's short for Paula Peaches. Who the car is named after."

"Who's *that*? That's the dumbest name I've ever heard. Who would name their kid that?"

"I'm pretty sure she named herself that." Rusty takes his beer back from me and finishes it in one gulp, then smiles. "Paula Peaches . . . is one of Texas's *finest* . . . actresses."

"I've never heard of her."

"No reason you should have." I can tell he's trying not to laugh.

I think about it, hard, then something dawns on me. "Is she"—I look around to make sure no one's listening and lower my voice to a whisper—"an *adult* actress?" I make air quotes around the word "adult."

Rusty gives a proud nod.

"That is so dirty! You guys were just . . . dirty . . . dirty guys."

Rusty grins like I just gave him a compliment. "Not as dirty as Paula Peaches."

Shana walks up to the table before I can think of something

clever to say back to him. "You two need another round?" She looks at me. "You doin' okay?" Of course I'm okay. Except I've been driving around in a dirty porn-star car.

"Yeesss," I say. "I would please like another round. But something fruity this time. With peaches, maybe."

Rusty snorts. I work to keep a straight face. Hard. Shana shakes her head and points at Rusty. "You better not get too drunk to dance. That's the only reason I let you in here."

She leans down and whispers to me like we're old friends. "J.D.'s not much of a dancer, so I have to get my fix from your boy here every once in a while. I hope you don't mind."

"I don't mind at all," I say. "But you better take him now." I scoot out of the booth and whisper to her this time. "Because I *think* we might be startin' to get drunk soon. And right now I gotta go pee. Where's your girls' room?"

Shana points, and I remember I've been there before. "Never mind." I smile. "I know where it is." I start to walk away but then turn around and point at the both of them. "You two. Go dance."

Rusty nods, and Shana winks, and as I weave my way across the dance floor to the bathroom, I decide I really, really like her. I like that she called Rusty my boy, and I wonder if she really thinks he is. 'Cuz he could be my boy, maybe. I don't know, I never thought of it. Well, that's not true. I thought of it when he saved us from crashing Paula, the dirty porn-star car, and when he was in his underwear in the monsoon. And then when we went swimming today and he jumped off that swing—

"Which guy are you talking about?" The voice startles me. Oh my god, was I actually talking out loud just then? I think

I might've been. There's a girl standing next to me holding a beer, and we're in line for the bathroom, and she looks really interested, and I'm pointing across the room to our booth. Holy crap, I'm drunk. "Um . . . nobody," I say quickly. "Nobody at all."

The bathroom door opens up, and I'm so glad it's my turn because I have to pee worse than I can ever remember. A girl comes out, then a guy trying to look all casual, and I give them a dirty look because they were probably making out in the bathroom, or worse, which is so dirty. I would never make out in a bathroom. Why's everyone so dirty?

I take care of my business as quick as I can, then check myself over in the mirror as I wash my hands. It's easier to see if I squeeze one eye shut, so I do, and I don't look half-bad. I look pretty good, in fact, and that's good, 'cuz it's time to find my boy and go dance. Ha. My boy.

Guitar and drums rush loud at me when I open the door, and everyone on the dance floor spins crazy and wild, and Rusty and Shana are right in the middle of it. And oh my god, she was right! How did I never know he could dance like that? He spins her fast, so her hair and the towel tucked in her back pocket both swing out behind her, then he ducks under her arm and turns her around so they're chest to chest for a second, all sexy and close, like the people on those dance shows.

I'm gonna dance with Rusty like that.

I walk out onto the dance floor and Shana sees me and waves me over, and when I get there, she puts Rusty's hand in mine. "Here. You take over," she says, out of breath. "I got a drink order, but he's just gettin' started." She winks, then smacks both our butts before she ducks off the dance floor and I lose her in the crowd.

Rusty grins, then bends down and puts his mouth so close to my ear I can feel his breath on my neck, and it gets me all tingly inside. "You ready to dance?" he asks. I nod. Oh yes, I'm ready to dance. He stands up with his eyes shining and his hair kind of tousled, and he's looking at me again with those eyes.

"All right. Just follow me, okay?" I nod again, and when he puts a hand on the small of my back and pulls me in close, I decide I'd follow him right into the bathroom to make out if he wanted to. It's so wrong, I know, but I've had enough tequila to make it seem a little bit right. I hope for a second I didn't just say that out loud, then decide so what if I did. I wouldn't take it back.

Rusty spins me out, then back in, and catches me, and we're moving across the floor, and I'm laughing because I really didn't know he could dance like this or that I wanted to kiss him so bad. I should do it right now, while we're dancing and I'm brave.

I try to think for a second, but I don't have time because we twist, back to back, arm over arm, then spin again, and now his hand's on my waist, and *wow* that's good. I'm gonna do it. I'm gonna kiss him the next time he pulls me in. Which should be any second, because I think I'm getting these dance steps. He throws me out again with one hand, and his other one comes out of nowhere and grabs me, pulls me around his back, and in one more twist . . . we're right there. Chest to chest. Closer than close. I lift my chin. He looks down at me. And it's now or never. I'm gonna kiss Rusty.

25

I'm gonna die, I know it.

Tequila was gonna be the death of me, no doubt. I lay still. Didn't dare move or even open my eyes just yet, because if I did either one, my head might honestly explode. Or I might throw up. Or both. I just lay there instead and tried to talk my body into going back to sleep for however long it would take for this feeling to go away. This had to be what death felt like. Either that or my first tequila hangover.

I almost gagged thinking about it. I'd taken that shot, and then Shana brought another one, and then . . . well . . . it had to have gone downhill from there, because everything after that was a series of fuzzy flashes: Wade Bowen up on stage . . . empty beer bottles and shot glasses all over the table . . . Rusty dancing with Shana . . . Rusty dancing with me. Me thinking it was a good idea to kiss Rusty . . .

Oh god.

I didn't. Did I?

I rubbed my forehead, trying to somehow pull the answer out of the haze that had settled there, but the harder I tried, the more my head pounded. Maybe my brain was trying to protect me from the answer. No matter that it hadn't bothered to remind me the night before what a bad idea kissing Rusty would be.

I rolled over and forced my eyes open. I was back in Celia and Bru's guest room, still in last night's clothes, boots and all. That was the sound of Bru and Rusty's voices drifting down the hall, and the smell of bacon cooking. And that sudden watery feeling in my mouth? That was my stomach warning me I was about to pay for last night. I jumped up and ran for the bathroom, faster than I would've thought I could in my current state, and made it just in time. Barely.

After, I rinsed my mouth out and took a good look in the mirror. Not only did I feel like hell, I looked it too, eyes all red and puffy, wild, tangly hair. And . . . was that . . . marker on my collarbone? I leaned forward and squinted at the backward writing in the mirror. Wade B. Wow. I had Wade Bowen sign me. I didn't know what was worse. That or the possibility I'd kissed Rusty. *Or* that I was gonna have to go out there and face him without knowing. *Oh, god.*

There was a soft knock on the door. "Honor? You all right in there, honey?" It was Celia.

"Yeah, I . . . was just about to get in the shower," I said as brightly as I could.

"Okay. Well, I'm going into town to run a few errands. Anything you need for the rest of the trip? The Fed Ex guy dropped off that part early this morning, and Rusty says he should have you back on the road to Kyra Kelley before noon."

"Really? That soon?" I thought I might throw up again. I knew we needed to get going, but the last thing I wanted to do today was hop back in the Pala and spend five or six uninterrupted hours with Rusty and a desert highway, even if we did make it and I got ahold of Kyra Kelley's assistant—I reached in my skirt pocket for Ashley's folded-up receipt with the number on it but came up empty. I patted and searched the other pockets with panicky hands. Nothing. *Oh, no. No, no, no.* I'd kept it on me since she gave it to me, a little piece of hope folded up in my pocket so I wouldn't lose it. But then I lost the entire night, and now—

"I was going to pick up some snacks for you two," Celia said through the door. "Anything else you need?"

That little piece of paper!

I strained against the fog in my memory, trying to figure out if I'd put it somewhere else—Celia's truck, maybe, or my purse. But I hadn't had one with me—so I slipped it into my pocket. That much I could remember.

"Honor? You sure you're all right in there?"

I shook my head at my pitiful reflection, then tried to suck it up even though I wanted to cry. And open the door and bury my face in her shoulder and tell her I wasn't near all right. That I'd lost my one chance to meet Kyra Kelley and tell her about Finn, like he asked me to do. The *one* thing he'd asked me to do. And now the one thing I'd failed at, all because I'd been trying to show off for Rusty. Thank god I hadn't had the tickets with me. Or his letter.

I tried to clear the regret lumped at the back of my throat. "I'm fine, thank you," I called through the door. "I'm just gonna get cleaned up." I reached out a shaky hand and turned on the water, hoping that was enough to send her on her way. Right now, all I wanted was a shower. And a magical cure for my own stupidity.

"Grease," Bru said, when I stepped into the kitchen. "Best cure for a hangover." He was sitting at the table, finishing up what had been a plate of eggs, bacon, and potatoes. Rusty stood at the stove with his back to me, pushing something around a pan with a spatula. I swallowed down my nausea.

"What about bad decisions?" I asked, pulling out a chair next to Bru. "Got a cure for those too?" Rusty turned around then with a smile that confirmed my fear that I hadn't just *thought* about kissing him. I dodged his eyes and turned to Bru. "I think I might've made a few last night."

Bru raised an eyebrow. "That one's a lot trickier." He looked from me to Rusty in a way that seemed like he'd added some things up, then sopped up the last of his runny egg yolk with a bit of toast. "Nothing easy for that. Humility, mostly." He wiped his mouth with a napkin and pushed his chair back from the table, then walked over to Rusty with his empty plate. "I gotta head out, but you can use whatever tools I got out there, all right?"

"Thank you," Rusty said.

Bru patted him on the arm. "And thank you for breakfast. That's the best cookin' I've had in a while. Truly." He grabbed his hat off the hook and put it on. "I'll be back before you go."

I nodded as Bru stepped out of the kitchen, leaving me

and Rusty alone, which was awkward in about eight different ways. He didn't look nearly as bad as I felt. Actually, he was all bright eyed and clean shaven. He walked over with two plates of picture-perfect breakfast and set one in front of me, then sat down across the table. I waited for it. For him to come out with some comment about me, and him. And me kissing him. He didn't, though. He just picked up his fork and used the edge of it to slice into his sunny-side-up egg.

I watched him chew and decided he was holding out to make me bring it up first. "I didn't know you could cook," I said, intent on not bringing it up at all.

"You didn't know I could dance, either, until last night." He smiled, then shoveled a bite of egg and potatoes into his mouth. There it was. I knew it. I did kiss him. He pointed with his empty fork at my plate. "You should eat something. It might help."

That would definitely not help. "No thanks," I said, pushing my plate away. "Still a little queasy over here." A new strategy for dealing with this whole thing occurred to me, and I tried to sound as casual as I could. "So . . . we must've had *a lot* to drink last night. I mean, I don't remember *anything*. I probably had no idea what I was doing."

Rusty laughed. "Oh, you knew what you were doing. Between the dancing on the stage and the body shot you took off Shana, you seemed like an old pro."

"*What?* Are you *serious*?" I needed to get up and run far, far away before this could get any worse.

Rusty almost choked on a laugh. I wished he would have. "Calm down, I'm just giving you a hard time."

I tried to be relieved. "So . . . I didn't, then . . . do those things?" Actually, those things might've been better than having kissed him.

Rusty smiled and took another bite, taking a long moment to chew and swallow before answering. "No," he said. "You didn't."

"Okay, good." I pulled my plate back toward me and picked up my fork like I might actually eat. "So . . ." I took a deep breath, braced myself for the worst. "What *did* I do? Besides have Wade Bowen autograph my chest?" Rusty's eyes went to the black smudge that peeked out of my tank top, and he smirked. Again. At me.

God, this was getting old. I was gonna have to suck it up and ask. Just get it over with, pride be damned. I rested the fork on my plate and leveled my tired eyes as best I could at Rusty, hating the question that was on the tip of my tongue. Then I stalled. "I need to ask you something."

Rusty sat forward and folded his hands on the table. "Ask away." He grinned.

I took a deep breath and let it out slow. "Okay. Um . . . did we kiss last night? Because if we did—if I kissed you . . . that was a big, tequila-filled mistake. Huge." I spread my hands wide in the air to show just how big. "Because I don't even think of you . . . it's just wrong, and I didn't mean it. I mean, if I did. Kiss you. Which I don't remember." I stabbed a potato and shoved it in my mouth to shut myself up and chewed it with plenty of humility.

Rusty looked at me like the question surprised him, then like he was entertained by the prospect, and I saw a tiny glimmer of hope. Maybe I hadn't. Maybe we'd just danced and I never tried. But now he knew I'd thought about it, or else why would I ask? *Damn it.* My head throbbed again.

He slowly put his feet up, one at a time, on the empty seat between us, then laced his fingers behind his head and leaned back, getting good and comfortable.

I wanted to punch him. "Rusty, come on."

"Tell me somethin', H," he said with a smile. "Did you *want* to kiss me last night?"

I didn't answer. This was fun for him, making me wonder. He was enjoying this whole thing.

"It's okay, you know, if you did," he continued. "You definitely wouldn't be the first girl to lose control of herself over me." He paused and looked right at me. "But then again . . . would you *really* want me to tell you if you did? 'Cuz you don't seem too happy about *that* prospect, either." He smirked. "Which probably *would* be a first."

"Rusty—" *How did I ever find him remotely attractive?*

"You seen my keys?" Celia asked as she walked in. She did a quick scan of the kitchen counter. Rusty motioned at the key rack near the door, which held a set that had to be hers. I poked my fork at the egg on my plate, trying to look like we weren't just having the discussion we'd been having. "Aw thanks, honey. I shoulda known. Bru always hangs them up for me." She gave me a once-over. "You sure you're okay, Honor?"

"Just fine, thank you," I muttered.

"We're good," Rusty said, smiling at me. "Just talkin' about how it's not proper to kiss and tell." He reached across the table and grabbed a piece of my bacon, crunching it as he stood. "You weren't gonna eat that, were you?"

I wondered what would happen if I threw my breakfast at

him right then. That probably wouldn't be very proper either. "No," I said, pushing my plate away. "Lost my appetite."

Rusty snorted and snapped up my other piece of bacon before he stacked our plates and took them to the sink. "I'm gonna go get that hose changed out, then give the dirty porn-star car a little tune-up before we get back on the road." He glanced over at me for a reaction, and I almost smiled at the flash of that conversation. Almost. Rusty leaned back against the counter. "You wanna give me a hand? So you know how to take care of your own car?"

"No. I don't." I turned to Celia. "You still have that stack of gossip magazines? I want to see if I can find out anything else about Kyra Kelley before we go." It was a hollow excuse, especially considering I had no illusions now that I would actually get to meet her. I had no idea where I could have left the phone number Ashley had given me. The best I could hope for at this point was that we'd make it to the show. I still had the tickets, at least, and now there was no way I could let Finn's gift be wasted. Not after what it must've taken him to get them.

Celia looped her jangly purse over her shoulder. "Sure thing, honey. They're all there in the living room. And I'll see if there's any new ones out when I'm in town, okay? I'll be back in a little bit."

"Thank you," I said, as sweet as I could. It wasn't her I was mad at.

Celia stepped out the door, leaving me in the kitchen with a splitting headache, a turning stomach, and the near certainty I'd lost all sense the night before and gone and kissed her son, who was now leaning against the counter looking amused as heck by the whole thing.

"Anything else you'll be needin', princess?" he asked.

"Yeah, actually, there is."

Rusty cocked his head. "And what's that?"

"I need for you to not talk to me right now." I slid my chair back from the table and stood to go. "This is starting to feel pointless, I feel like I got run over by a truck, and I don't want any crap from you about it, okay?"

His face fell just a little, but he was quick to recover. "Fine with me," he said. "I'll be outside. Fixing *your* car. For *your* trip." He ducked out the door, then shut it with a force that hammered at my temples.

My trip. That's what Finn had meant it to be when he sent me that letter. But when I got in the Impala and pointed it at California, I'd wanted it to be *our* trip. Mine and Finn's. I'd wanted to take his car and his letter and that pinch of dust and give him something impossible in return. A send-off he'd be proud of, no matter how crazy it sounded.

All I'd done, though, was go off course—miles and miles from where I should have been, and I didn't know where to begin to find my way back now.

26

"I don't have a map," Celia said, "but this should get you there." She handed me a MapQuest printout. "It says it should take around seven hours, so you'll make it there by this evening." She squeezed my arm. "I'm so happy for you, honey. Your brother would be proud of you doing this for him."

"Thank you." I didn't argue, just set the papers down on the passenger seat and squinted at her in the bright sunlight that made my head ache even worse.

"You're welcome, but it's me who should be thanking you." She hugged me to her tiny frame, and I tried not to stiffen.

"Why?" I asked, pulling away as gently as I could.

She glanced toward the garage, where Rusty was talking with Bru, then motioned for me to lean in. "Just that you . . . and this trip . . . it's good for Rusty. He took the news about Finn so hard I thought it might break him in two, I really did. Lord knows he's got his daddy's tendencies to deal with things with a bottle. Which is just what he started to do. His energy was so dark for a while there . . ." She glanced at him with eyes that were tender and wet with emotion. "But once he worked things out about you, and about that promise he made to Finn, it gave him something important to focus on, something that mattered, you know?"

I didn't, actually. I hadn't realized I was just a chore to look after, or a way for Rusty to feel important. I tried to push away all the implications of what she'd just said to me: that Finn had thought I needed looking after but left anyway, that he'd decided Rusty was the one to do it even though he couldn't look after himself most the time, that I was still somehow on the outside of their friendship, even now.

"Honor," Celia said, putting her hand on my shoulder, "I know he can be hard to handle. I do. Which is why I'm thanking you—for being someone worth enough to him to help him through. And for being gracious enough to let him take this journey with you."

I looked at the ground, not wanting her to see how wrong I thought she was, wishing I could bite my tongue just a little longer, but it was no use. "This isn't some spiritual journey," I said. "This is the biggest mistake I've ever made." It felt rotten to say, but it was true. "I was supposed to be at school a day ago, touring campus with everyone else," I went on. "I took off the day after they put Finn in the ground, lied to my aunt, and haven't spoken to my best friend since I left. And for what? So I could go to California to see Kyra Kelley's last show? And hope I got a chance to talk to her about my dead brother who sent me the tickets?" I stood there clinging to anger because it was easier, right then, than facing up to everything else I felt. "This is not a journey. This is just . . ."

Celia smiled gently at me like I hadn't just let loose on her, then put her arms around me and held me there, all wrapped up in reassurance and the scent of rose oil. She spoke softly, through my hair. "I think this—you . . . and Rusty . . . going to the concert . . . it's part of something bigger for you. We all do crazy things, and sometimes they don't make sense until we've seen them through, but this—this is something you need to see through. I know it. So you go, like your brother said, and—"

"And what?" Rusty asked as he walked up. He didn't wait for Celia to answer, just looked right to me. "You 'bout ready to go? Better pee now, 'cuz I'm not stopping till we're halfway there."

I felt Celia's eyes on me, trying to finish what she'd been saying, and I was thankful for an excuse to walk away. She'd brushed awfully close to a lot of things I didn't want to think about. Already having failed Finn being the biggest one.

"I'll be right back," I said, excusing myself. My boots crunched over the red-rock driveway back to the house, almost loud enough to cover up Celia murmuring something to Rusty about being careful with me.

When I came back out a few minutes later, I'd swallowed everything down enough to say our official, polite thank-yous and good-byes to Celia and Bru out by the car. I didn't argue when Rusty walked around to the driver's side and got in. If he wanted to drive, that was fine with me. I'd sleep all the way to California and then figure out what to do when we got there. I ducked into the passenger seat and pulled the door shut after me.

Bru bent down to the open window. "You two have a safe trip. And keep your ears open for the universe." He winked. "Sometimes it whispers."

"Okay." I smiled. But I was sure it didn't have anything else to say to me. I'd already wasted my cosmic grace.

He stood and gave the hood a pat, Rusty turned the key in the ignition, and I sat back against the already hot vinyl seat, shoring myself up for the next seven hours.

"So you're really not gonna talk to me this entire drive, huh?"

"No," I said, eyes trained on the ugly, endless nothingness of the landscape outside. We'd made it a surprisingly long time in silence—across the California border, and now we were somewhere in the middle of more desert. "Nothing to talk about." Why would I want to talk about how I was just a favor Rusty was taking care of for my brother? Or how it turned out to be true that I really couldn't take care of myself? What I wanted was to stay mad about it, because maybe then those things wouldn't hurt so much.

He turned down the music. "C'mon, Honor. I've known enough girls to know that means there's plenty you wanna talk about. Why don't you just yell at me for somethin' and get it over with?"

I looked over, and he did too for a second before we both looked away again.

"Aren't you supposed to be at Hell Week or something? Why are you even here?" I said it more to my window than to Rusty, but I felt him shift in the seat.

"Why are *you* here?" he countered. "You're supposed to be in Austin, going to school, being a big success, making it worth it."

"Making what worth it?"

Rusty didn't answer.

I looked out the dusty window. "I don't know why I'm here with you. It's not like Finn made me promise to look after you or anything. At least he had faith in you." Out the corner of my eye, I saw Rusty glance over at me again, but I kept my eyes on the solid yellow line that went on forever next to us.

He sighed. "It wasn't like that, H. Stop feeling sorry for yourself. I'm not babysitting you. I got drunk and passed out in your car. And then I woke up in New Mexico."

"You could've stayed in Sedona. Or you could've turned us around today, back to Texas."

"You want me to turn around, I will. Say the word." Rusty slowed the car like he was gonna pull over. "I've had about enough of you as you've probably had of me, but the road back home is a lot longer right now than the road to the coast, and I'd rather make it all the way to the ocean today than end up back in Big Lake tomorrow. If that's all right with you."

The ocean. I'd almost forgotten about it. Seeing Kyra Kelley seemed like a more ridiculous idea every time I thought of it, but the ocean didn't. I thought of Finn's letter, and how he'd said to go on a trip and put my feet in the ocean. Rusty wasn't Lilah, but he had a point. We'd come this far already. "How far away are we?"

"Couple hours."

"Fine," I said, climbing into the backseat. "Wake me up when we get there."

27

"Hey. We're here."

Rusty cut the engine. I creaked one eye open enough to see the dotted ceiling of the Pala, or Paula, or whatever we were calling it (her) now. "I don't have to pee, okay? Keep going." I rubbed both eyes with the heels of my hands and blinked away what felt like only a few minutes' sleep.

"No, we're *here*." Rusty grinned back at me, then turned around and looked out the windshield, shaking his head. "I'll be damned."

I sat up quick and looked around, trying to get my bearings. We were parked on the side of the highway, in front of a small yellow building with white trim and a sign on the front that read THE SHAKE SHACK. To the side of it was a big blue deck with a giant postcard-perfect palm tree right in the center, its fronds sticking up against the dusky sky like crazy morning hair.

"We're *here* here? Oh my god!" I yanked on the metal handle and gave the door a nudge with my shoulder, just as Rusty did the same thing from the front seat. And then we both stepped out into balmy, warm air that smelled like nothing I'd ever smelled before. And then I heard it. Above the sound of the cars zooming by on the highway, I heard a loud crash, a staticlike rush, and then another crash.

Rusty's eyes met mine for an instant, and I saw in them the same glee that I felt right then. Without having to say anything, we both hopped up the steps onto the deck, and I realized we were high on a bluff. And spread out below us, vast, and huge, and sparkling, was the ocean. I didn't know whether to laugh or cry.

I'd seen it in movies plenty of times. Run my eyes over the blue of it in pictures and posters, and tried to imagine what it would really feel like to be there. And now there it was, right in front of me, loud and alive and real. I wanted to capture that moment, that feeling of seeing something so very big, and so beautiful, it made my heart want to burst right open.

Neither one of us spoke for a long time. We just stood there, side by side, and stood there, and kept standing there, trying to take it in. The fiery ball of a sun melted into the horizon, throwing pink and orange light that broke into a thousand tiny diamonds when it hit the water. Far below us, the sand glinted slick and shiny and inviting. The happy voices of a couple of kids playing in the water drifted up on the breeze, and I watched as the boy took the little girl's hand and they ran together, away from a wave that crumbled into white foam in front of them. After a long moment full of too many feelings to sort out, I grabbed Rusty's arm. "C'mon. Let's go put our feet in the ocean."

A slow smile, a real one, crept across his face. "I saw some stairs over there when I pulled in." He headed down the steps and toward a path lining the bluff. I lingered a second, not quite ready to take my eyes off the water or let go of the feeling that this was one of those tiny moments that turned out to be one of the big ones later on.

"You comin'?" Rusty called. He was on the path already, barefoot and smiling like a little boy.

"Yeah, I'm coming." I swept my eyes over the water again, all the way to the horizon, before turning to go with him, and a warm kind of peace spread out in me. I kissed it into my fingertips, then blew it into the breeze, a silent thank-you swirling its way up to Finn.

We sat on the sand, feet and legs glistening with salty water in the leftover glow from the sun. Just as the last sliver of it dipped into the ocean, we'd put our toes in the water and let it splash cool and foamy up our legs, laughing together with a lightness we hadn't had since we were kids. No hurt feelings or undercurrents of complications. Just true, simple happiness. Rusty leaned back on his elbows, watching the waves line up, then break, and I raked lines in the sand with my fingers, wondering at the fact that we'd really made it all the way to the beach.

"Hey, Rusty?" I said suddenly, "I'm sorry about how I acted earlier today. I just . . ."

He turned to me, eyebrow raised. "Woke up on the wrong end of a tequila bottle?"

"Yeah." I laughed, feeling more than a little sheepish, but happy he wasn't one to hold a grudge. "I guess I did. I'm sorry."

Rusty waved it off. "Been there plenty of times."

"And I wanted to say thank you. For getting us here. To the ocean. I think Finn would be happy."

"Yeah." He nodded but didn't seem to be paying attention anymore.

I followed his gaze, expecting to see a hot girl in a bikini, but instead I saw a big crowd of people walking up the beach toward us. And not just any people. Most of them had their heads bowed, and they all carried what looked, from a distance, like white boxes. An elderly Japanese man dressed in a long yellow robe held a torch, and in between the crash of the waves, his voice drifted toward us, singing or chanting words I didn't understand.

I looked around for cameras or something. Maybe they were filming a movie? We were close to LA and Hollywood and all that.

We kept watching as the group, a mix of all ages, made its way to the mouth of a wide creek near us that emptied lazily into the ocean. The leader—priest, I guessed, stopped at the edge of it and waited quietly as they gathered around him. I looked away because it felt a little like intruding to keep watching, but Rusty was watching them intently, and the few other people on the beach had gathered to do the same, so I brought my eyes back to where they stood.

The old man started up again, now close enough that I could hear the age in his voice. And when he spoke, I was surprised it was in English. "Welcome," he said, spreading his arms wide. "We are here, on this final evening of Obon, to honor the loved ones we've lost and the ancestors who came before us." He paused and swept his eyes over the ocean. "Our tradition tells us that humans come from the water, and so tonight, we will return the spirits of our families to the sea. Each lantern we set afloat will carry a departed spirit from our shore, where they passed their lives, to the horizon of peace and redemption, where they will rest." He turned toward the real horizon, then back to the people gathered around him and bowed. "The sun has set. Let us begin."

A tiny woman, bent over from age, stepped from the crowd and began to sing, soft words I didn't understand, but the feeling behind them was something I did. Rusty and I watched quietly as the first person, a middle-aged man, stepped forward to the priest. He lit the candle inside the man's lantern, then spoke a name before bending gently to the water with it. When he opened his hands, the lantern trembled a tiny bit before it caught the edge of the current and drifted placidly toward the ocean. The priest repeated the same motions for each lantern, lighting the candle, speaking the name, and setting the lantern adrift down the creek and out to sea.

It was beautiful, and as I watched, I wished Finn's memorial had felt this way, so much more soft and peaceful than the sternness of his military funeral. The rifle shots and the trumpet, the general's words and the flag—all those things were meant to honor and pay tribute to him and his service. But they didn't bring the sort of peace that this seemed to bring the people who set the little lights afloat. The lanterns spread out, flickering over the water in the calm of the evening, and it seemed like the way saying good-bye to someone ought to feel—like you were setting them free so they could always be out there somewhere. It was a wholly different feeling than watching the shiny black casket be lowered slowly into the ground. My eyes swept the sky like a reflex.

Rusty and I sat and watched for who knows how long as each individual lantern was lit, then set free. We watched until the very last person stepped up to the priest. She was a little girl, maybe six years old, and he had to bend low to light her candle. She bowed her head solemnly as he did, but when he reached for her lantern, she shook her head and hugged it tighter. Carefully, she knelt down and set it in the sand, then reached into her pocket and brought out a rolled-up piece of paper tied with a string. She gave it a kiss, looped the end of the string around the corner of the lantern, and stood slowly with it. But she didn't give it to the priest then. Instead, she held up her chin and stepped toward the edge of the creek, and in a small, quavery voice, spoke the name of her person before she set the lantern into the current herself.

It got very quiet as we all watched it drift down to the ocean to join the others floating peacefully out to sea, their tiny lights shimmering into the night. I watched hers for as long as I could, wishing I'd had the courage and grace to stand up at Finn's funeral and send him off in my own way, with a speech or a letter or some tiny gesture that was as sweet and earnest as what she'd just done.

After a while, the breeze picked up and the air got so cool I had to wrap my arms around my knees to stay warm. Slowly, in twos and threes, the crowd of people separated and drifted back up the beach, stopping every so often to point out to the ocean, where the tiny lights were now spread far and wide like constellations over the water. And the whole time, Rusty didn't move or speak. He just sat back next to me in the sand, and I wished I knew what he was thinking about. Asking him wouldn't do anything but ruin it, so I didn't say anything either.

It wasn't until the little girl and her family left that he finally sat up and looked over at me. "You hungry or cold? You wanna go back up to the car?"

I shook my head, scared that if I tried to talk, something in me might come unhinged.

"Okay," he said like he understood. "We'll stay a while longer then."

He took my hand and held it in both of his, and we sat there that way on the dark beach until the last tiny twinkle of the lanterns was just a golden speck. By the time we made it back up the stairs to the Pala, we were both worn out and spent from the day, so when Rusty pulled us into an empty lot along the bluff and parked next to the little kiosk, I didn't argue. Wordlessly, we climbed into the back and arranged our clothes and the one sleeping bag I'd brought into a decent enough bed for us to sleep on. Any other day, I probably would've made a big deal about sending him to sleep in the front seat, far away from me.

But tonight I didn't care about any of that. Tonight I wanted to be close to him—not in *that* kind of way, but in the kind of way that made me feel less alone and less sad. The kind of way I hoped could help him, too. So when he slid under the sleeping bag, near enough for me to feel the warmth coming off his skin, I moved near enough to cuddle up and hoped he would understand. He shifted and brought his arm around my shoulders, pulling me in even closer, and I laid my head down on his chest and closed my eyes to everything but the steady rise and fall of his chest and the solid thump of his heart.

28

The first knock on the window woke me up enough to realize it was morning. At the second knock, I rolled over and figured out that the heavy weight across my chest was Rusty's arm, which was enough to startle me upright just in time to see the officer lean down and peer in the window before knocking on it again. *Oh, god.* He saw me see him and said, from the other side of the glass, "Miss, would you please step out of the car?"

I nodded in a panic, then shook Rusty hard. "Wake up! There's a cop outside!" *What do we do, what do we do, what do we do?*

"Take it easy," he said, rubbing his eyes. "They probably just want us to move the car or somethin'." He lay there a minute, blinking up at the ceiling like it was no big deal there was a cop outside the window asking us to get out. Or that I had completely snuggled up to him the night before.

The cop knocked again. "Miss?"

"One second," I called brightly, hoping being nice would earn me brownie points. "Come *on*," I said pulling on Rusty's arm. "I'm not getting out by myself."

Finally, he sat up and squinted out the window. "All right, I'm comin'. Gimme a sec."

"We don't have a sec. Hurry up." I smoothed my hair back as if that would somehow make a better impression on the policeman. Rusty finally sat up and nodded at me, and we each opened our door. "Hi," I said, a little too chipper, to the officer who stood by my door.

He was younger looking than I'd expected, and cute, with buzzed blond hair and bright blue eyes that stood out against the morning gray. "Good morning." He nodded, then looked past me as Rusty stepped out on his side.

"Mornin' officer," he said, running a hand through his hair and wearing his best Big Tex grin. "Is there a problem?"

The officer—S. Chase, according to his name tag, opened his mouth to answer but was interrupted by a snort from a second officer walking up behind him. He was older and taller and had that pompous air about him you can just sense on some people. He adjusted his belt, and as he got to us, chest all puffed out with his own authority, he planted his feet firmly, like he planned on staying awhile.

"'Is there a problem?'" He laughed like he'd just cracked a joke and looked to Officer Chase like he should too. "That's a new one, huh?" He turned his attention to Rusty and spoke with a smile that was anything but friendly. "Of course there's a problem. *Otherwise* . . . we wouldn't be knocking on your window this fine morning. Would we?"

I looked to Officer Chase for help. "We're contacting you because it's illegal to camp overnight in this parking lot," he said simply.

"Oh. We . . ."

I didn't know what to say, but Rusty stepped in with his manners turned up a notch higher than I'd ever seen. "I apologize, sir, we weren't aware of that. We'll head out right away."

The other one shook his head, and the sun glinted off its shiny, bald surface. "Oh, you weren't *aware*? Can't you read? Because you parked directly in front of the sign that says 'No Overnight Camping Permitted,' see?" He pointed and, sure enough, below the money-collecting window of the kiosk was a sign saying exactly that. "So no. You won't be heading out. First we'll need to see your IDs and the registration for this vehicle."

Rusty's jaw tightened, but he didn't drop his smile. "All right, sure."

We opened up the two front doors and leaned in to dig for our wallets. Rusty slid his license easily out of his, then opened the glove box. "Registration in here?"

"I think so. . . . I don't know. . . ." I fumbled with the plastic pocket of my wallet, trying to get my license out.

Rusty looked at me, serious. "What do you mean, you don't know? Where'd you put it?"

"I mean . . . I don't think I *got* it?"

A bad, sinking feeling started in my stomach, and it got worse when Rusty stopped what he was doing and asked me slowly, "Did you pay the registration for the car this year?"

"No. *I* never did. I thought Finn took care of all that

stuff. . . . I . . . oh, no." I stood up, knocking my head on the door frame in the process.

"You okay, miss?" Officer Chase asked.

"Yeah." I handed him my license, then rubbed the back of my head. "Here's this. Um, about the registration—"

"It's nine months overdue," the mean one interrupted. "I ran it already. You know what that means, sweetheart?"

"What?" I asked sharply. I was starting to hate this guy a little more every time he opened his mouth. I looked to Officer Chase. "Do I have to pay a big fine or something?"

"It means we have to tow it," he said grimly. "It can't be on the road when it's that long overdue."

"You can't tow it! We're eight hundred miles from *home.*" I willed myself not to cry. "It was my brother's car, and he was over in Iraq, and I didn't know I was supposed to register it, and he . . ."

Rusty cut in. "Look, her brother just passed away, and I'm sure we can get it all straightened out once we get back home, if you could please just cut us a break this time."

Officer Chase shook his head. "I'm sorry, but I can't."

I tried not to panic completely. "What can we do, then?" I asked, on the edge of tears. This couldn't be happening.

His partner pressed his thin lips together and furrowed his brow like he pitied me. "Well, the first thing *you* can do, Miss . . ."—he peered over Chase's shoulder at my license—"Lindsey, is accept responsibility for your actions. Says right here you're almost eighteen—"

"Oh, *come* on," Rusty said, stepping in front of me. "If you're gonna be a dick and take the car, we don't need a speech, too."

"Easy there, cowboy. Somebody needs to tell it like it is." The old snake of an officer snapped his eyes back to me. "The *second* thing you can do, sweetheart, *Honor*, is to show some respect for your brother's memory by taking care of his things and getting this car up to date."

"All right, that's enough," Chase said, glaring at his partner. "Let's go call it in."

My heart pounded in my chest as they walked back across the parking lot to the patrol car. I'd never hated anyone so much in my life as I hated that police officer right then. I wanted to scream.

"That guy's an asshole," Rusty said, putting his hand on my shoulder. "We'll get it figured out. It'll be okay."

"No, Rusty, it *won't*!" I snapped. "It's not gonna be okay, because *you* parked us overnight right in front of a sign that says no overnight parking!" I twisted away from him and shook my head. "And then you mouthed off to that guy, so now he's gonna take Finn's *car*." I was crying now, angry tears that slid fast and hot down my cheeks.

Rusty's jaw tightened, and he took a step toward me, his voice low. "You need to calm down right now. This is *not* my fault."

"Yes it is," I spit back at him. "They wouldn't *be* here if you hadn't parked here. If you'd actually read the sign." I looked up at it, deciding to ignore the fact that I hadn't either. He'd been the one driving. Across the parking lot, the two officers stood on the far side of their car, looking like they were having an argument too.

"Yeah, Honor? What about the registration? Finn's been gone over a year now. You didn't think to check up on that?"

"Now you're agreeing with *that* guy? *I* need to be more responsible?" I shook my head and laughed at the absurdity of it. "You're one to talk, Rusty. You went off to the college Finn was supposed to go to and became even more of a drunk than you were in high school. You got a chance that he missed out on, and you blew it." I didn't have to look at him to know I'd hurt him. I turned my back instead and stared across the highway at the gray fog that hid the ocean. "Why don't you just leave? Leave like he did. It was no problem for him, so it shouldn't be one for you."

Rusty's voice was thick with anger. "Is that what you really think? That he just left you?"

I didn't answer. I didn't know what to think.

When Rusty spoke next, his voice came out flat. "Wow, Honor," he said from behind me. "There's a whole lot you don't see." He stepped around in front of me so I had to face him. "Maybe that cop is right, you know? Maybe it's time for you to grow up and hear the truth, which is that you have no idea how to take care of yourself because Finn looked out for you your whole damn life."

"Shut up."

"No, there's something else you should know, if you wanna talk about the truth." He paused, then looked at me with eyes that flashed fierce with anger. "He didn't give up a full ride and join the marines because he all of a sudden got patriotic."

Something in me stilled, even though my heart pounded in my throat. "What are you talking about?"

"You know what a full ride means, Honor? It means he was going to school for free. To play football. Just like he wanted. He didn't miss out on that chance, he gave it up. Changed his mind. For you. So he could pay for you to go to your stupid little dream school."

"What are you even *talking* about?" I shook my head, took a step back. "I had money. Our parents left us money."

"No they didn't. Finn just told you that. Right after that trip you guys took to Austin, and you came back all bent on going there and nowhere else. You had your head so far up your ass about that, like you just assumed you could go wherever you wanted. So he figured out a way to make it happen for you, like he always did. You know what that was? Joining the marines for a paycheck and telling you your parents left you a college fund."

"You're a liar," I said through gritted teeth.

Rusty snorted. "That's one thing you've called me that I'm not." He turned to walk away, then paused and leveled his eyes right at me. "I wish I was. But the truth is, him leaving— it's all on you." With that, he turned his back on me.

I sank down to the ground right where I'd been standing, hands on my head like they could block out what he said. But it was too late. Those words had already gone straight in and twisted up my insides into a knot of anger and guilt and ugliness. *How could Finn have done that?* I never would have said yes to that. And he never gave me a choice.

Beside my foot was a rock the size of my fist, and I wrapped my fingers around it and squeezed until my knuckles went white. Then I stood up with it heavy in my hand, wanting to break something.

And I did.

I brought my arm back and hurled it with all the force in me at the stupid No Parking sign bolted to the front of the kiosk that started this whole mess, but the throw was wild. The window above the sign exploded into a thousand jagged shards that clattered down onto the asphalt like glass rain. My breath left me. Rusty jumped and turned around, looking from me to the broken window. The two officers snapped to attention and started walking over quick, hands on their radios. And I stood there, out of breath, not feeling any better, but not wishing for a second that I could take it back either.

"Which one of you idiots threw that rock?" Officer Asshole boomed from a few paces away. He looked from me to Rusty, then back to me. I narrowed my eyes at him and got ready to tell him where to shove it. What did it matter now anyway?

And then Rusty laughed—a bitter laugh that sounded like trouble. I looked over as he put his hands in his pocket and stepped casually toward the officers. "I did, you jackass." He motioned up at the kiosk. "Screw your stupid sign."

Oh, no.

They looked at me like they didn't believe him, like they knew just as well as I did that he hadn't thrown the rock. And I wanted to say so, I did, but I just stood there dumb and frozen and in shock.

"What?" Rusty said, keeping his hands in his pockets. "You need an instant replay to do your job?" He turned his head to the side and spit. "Come on now, Officer Dick . . ." He pretended to squint at his name tag. "What does that say?"

Oh god, Rusty, don't.

"Okay, Tex." Officer Dixon smiled. "Have it your way." In less time than it took me to open my mouth and try to set things straight, he had Rusty turned around with his cheek shoved up against the Pala and his hands behind his back.

"You're under arrest for vandalism and destruction of state property." He reached to his belt and pulled out a set of shiny handcuffs, snapped one neatly on each of Rusty's wrists, and squeezed them tight.

This is not happening.

"Little tight there, officer," Rusty said through gritted teeth.

Dixon yanked him off the car and smiled. "That's the best thing I've heard all day." He turned Rusty around and started to walk him over to the patrol car, but then he paused and yelled over his shoulder to Officer Chase. "You got her?"

How can this be happening?

"Yeah, I got it," Chase said. He turned to me with a look that seemed like he felt bad. "Anything you need out of your car before we take it? Purse? Wallet? Phone?" I hadn't even noticed the tow truck pull up. I could barely breathe, let alone talk.

This really cannot be happening.

The driver got out and nodded to Officer Chase, who nodded back. Given the okay, he hopped up on the flat metal bed of his truck, unrolled a chain from somewhere, and walked it down to the Pala. To Finn's car—the only thing I had left here and the last I had of him. I watched, horrified into silence, as he hooked it up.

What was there to say? That I was an awful, selfish person who'd been completely clueless about what other people were willing to do for me? That Rusty getting arrested, and Finn's car getting taken away, and Finn joining the marines and dying were all things that happened because of *me*? Because everyone thought I needed to be taken care of?

Officer Chase must've thought so too, because before the

tow truck driver turned on the winch to roll the car up onto the platform and take it away, he went and pulled my purse out. He handed it over like he pitied me, then gave me his card and the number of the impound yard. I took it numbly, without saying thank you, then walked away from him and sat on the curb, more pitiful than I'd ever been in my life.

The tow truck driver handed Officer Chase a clipboard to sign, and that was it. He got back in his truck and took Finn's car away from me. Officer Chase glanced at me one last time, then he turned and walked over to the car, where his partner waited with Rusty handcuffed in the back of it. Because of me.

I couldn't even look at him as they drove by because I hated myself so much for not standing up for him like he had for me. The thing I hated most, though, was the question repeating itself over and over in my head, because it was a selfish one that just confirmed everything Rusty had said about me. *What am I supposed to do now?*

29

I saw Rusty's face in my mind as they drove away. How angry he'd been with me in one second, angry enough to hurt me the same as I had him, but then how, in the very next instant, he'd come to my defense. Saved me. And now, as I sat there on the curb watching cars come and go through the parking lot, another truth smacked me hard. There was no one left to save me. I was utterly alone, and it was undeniably my fault.

I stood, thinking that walking might help me sort out how I'd gone from coming to see Kyra Kelley's farewell concert, and telling her about Finn, to sitting here alone in California, with his letter in my purse, Rusty in jail, and the Pala taken away. It was a crazy, tangled mess, but that didn't surprise me, because honestly, I was too. *How had I been so wrapped up in myself, I didn't realize what was going on? How had Finn given up everything for me without me even knowing? Or giving me a choice?*

How had I just stood there and let Rusty take the blame and go to jail for me? How had I gotten here, to this place, where everything was wrong and it all came back to me?

I didn't know how to begin facing those questions, or if I even wanted to, so I kept walking until I came to the highway, then pushed the button for the crosswalk. The green man flashed on the light, and I crossed the highway to the ocean side and found a path that rolled and wound along the bluff above the water. It seemed as good as any, considering my current situation, so I set foot down it, hoping it would lead to the sand and the water, where I'd found a little bit of peace before things went so wrong in so many ways.

As soon as I stepped onto the path, two nearly identical blond ladies blew by me from the opposite direction, talking and laughing and speed-walking two paces too fast for their little dogs, who trailed behind. The sight of them, two girlfriends chatting together, made me think of Lilah and what she would say about this whole thing. She was off at orientation, with no idea I'd gotten in Finn's car and driven all the way out here. With Rusty.

I almost smiled at the thought, because that'd be the first thing she'd be curious about—what it was like to spend so much time with him in the cab of the Pala. She'd want to know all the tiny details. I thought about which ones I'd tell her, where I'd even start. Maybe with how he ended up in the car with me in the first place, all drunk and angry. Or how on that first night in the campground he'd been mean enough to make me cry, or how he talked crude or tried to pee into my empty soda cup or drove in his underwear. Those would be the things she'd expect to hear, because they fit into what we'd both thought of him for so long. But none of that mattered now.

No. If I could call her right now and tell her anything, I'd tell her he was better than I'd thought. That I understood why Finn had loved him so much, because in spite of everything else, he was the kind of friend any of us would be lucky to have. The kind that looked out for you when you needed it and backed off when you needed it. And the kind who told you the truth when you needed that, even if it hurt. I couldn't be angry at him for what he'd told me. I hadn't just been yelling at Rusty about the sign. I'd unloaded everything on him—everything I was mad about, everything that seemed unfair, everything that hurt, because I wanted someone to blame for it all. And now I had only myself.

I put my head down and followed the curve of the path, not ready to think about that or Finn or the choices he'd made and what they meant. I couldn't. Instead, I walked and walked until I came to a lookout place at the edge of the bluff, high above the ocean. It was foggy down below, so foggy I couldn't even see the water that had sparkled for miles in every direction the day before. It was like it was gone, just the same as everything else that had been good in my life.

At that moment I wanted more than anything to see it again, and feel that big bursting feeling I'd had standing there looking at the ocean with Rusty, before I'd gone and ruined everything. I stood there forever, squinting through the fog, trying to get it back, but I knew I couldn't. Perfect moments like that couldn't be repeated. And horrible ones, like my argument with Rusty in the parking lot, couldn't be taken back. I hoped, though, that I could somehow make it right.

I glanced around, and my eyes found a narrow trail that zigzagged down the bluff, into the fog. It had to lead down to the sand and the water. I could walk the beach and find where we'd been the day before, where I'd seen some buildings and maybe there'd be a payphone. I'd call Gina and tell her everything. And she'd be angry with me, but she'd know what to do, and she'd help me get Rusty out of jail and get Finn's car back, and then . . . Well. I hadn't figured out what then, but at least I had something to think about doing now.

I climbed, one leg at a time, over the rope that bordered the lookout and made my way down the steep trail, slipping more than a time or two on the loose rocks, and using the bushes along the sides to hold on to. By the time I made it to the sand, the back of my skirt was the same shade of brown as the trail and my hands smelled like sage brush, but I felt a little better already. I could smell the salt and hear the crash of the little waves, and even though I couldn't see the ocean stretch out forever to the horizon, I could feel a twinge of that same expansive feeling from the day before. The water was a soft shade of gray in the morning fog, and the way it rolled up over the sand and then back was so calm and steady, I wanted to sit and watch it forever.

I sat down and pulled my boots off, then dug my toes into the cool of the sand and looked around. The beach was littered with all kinds of things—sticks and seaweed, a red plastic shovel, a few bits of shells here and there, all in a wavy line, like the ocean had washed them up then receded. I hoped none of the things were last night's lanterns. I hoped they'd all made it to the horizon of peace and redemption, like the priest had said, or that they were still out there somewhere, their little lights twinkling through the fog. I hoped that little girl's message had made it where it was supposed to go.

The thought struck me as ironic as soon as I had it, because it seemed like no matter where you thought you were supposed to be, life had other ideas. I was supposed to be at orientation today, getting ready to start my whole new life off at college, yet here I was, alone on the beach, all the way in California. And Rusty, he should be at football practice, getting yelled at by the coach for being a smart-ass but making a name for himself because he's the best they've got.

And Finn . . .

He should be here, seeing the ocean with me. He should've been in the car with the windows down, singing "Wayward Son" with Rusty, and driving through the wavy desert heat. And he should've seen the sun rise from beneath the water in New Mexico and the stars streak white and sparkling over the red rocks in Arizona. Because the only reason I'd done any of those things was him and his "real letter" and the tickets he'd sent. *Put your feet in the ocean,* he'd said. *Tell Kyra Kelley about your handsome older brother.*

Her final show was in a few hours, and I was going to miss it. I'd made it all this way, and still, I wouldn't see it. Not a chance I'd be able to tell her about Finn.

I watched the waves pitch up, then tumble down into foam, and thought how this thing was never really about going to see Kyra Kelley's last concert, let alone telling her about him. If he were alive, that's all the trip would have been about. But once he was gone, I'd used his gift as a reason to take his car and just go away from the truth of it for a little while. I'd put my feet in the ocean like he wanted me to, but he'd never know all the other things he'd given me.

Or maybe he could. Maybe I could tell him.

I opened up my purse and dug around, then came up with the only paper in there—Finn's crinkled letter. I opened the pages in my lap, smoothed out the creases as best I could, thinking about what I wanted to say back to him. I didn't need to think about it long, though. When I took the pen from my purse and pressed the tip to the blank side of the first page, words came fast and I poured it all out.

I told Finn he'd been crazy to do what he did for me, and that I never would've let him give up everything for me to go to UTA if I'd known. I told him I was mad that he'd lied to do it but that I understood why, because he'd been protecting me our whole life. And now that I knew the truth, it was gonna stick with me for the rest of mine. But then I told him I was glad I knew what he'd done, because I wouldn't have to wonder about all the whys anymore. He hadn't enlisted for some reason none of us would ever understand. He'd done it for me. Because he thought it was the right thing to do. I told him I admired him for that and for everything he'd done and been, and that Rusty was right when he said that some people are just better than the rest of us.

Then I told him I found out Rusty was that way too. I told him how Rusty had stuck by me since the funeral, in spite of losing his best friend and knowing I'd been the reason. How he'd taken my Kyra Kelley idea and seen me through the desert and the pouring rain and more desert, all the way to the ocean. I told him about the rope swing and our tequila night (minus the kiss), and how I knew the joke about the Pala now. And I told him he'd be proud of Rusty for all of it. Especially what he'd done for me that morning.

I don't know how long I sat there writing, but I covered his letter and the backs of the tickets with all my thank-yous and sorries and memories, all my sadness and gratitude and hope. And at the end, before I said my good-bye, I promised my brother I'd be as good as he had been and I'd make sure that what he'd done for me was worth it.

When I finished, I folded it up, matched my creases with his, and sat quiet a few moments, listening to the sound of the waves and breathing in the salt air. Writing a letter wasn't gonna change or fix anything, I knew that. But it felt good to lay it all out there, all the things I'd felt and wanted to say but hadn't been able to until now.

I stood and tucked the letter in my back pocket, not exactly sure what I wanted to do with it yet. The sun had melted the fog just down the beach, and patches of warm light spread out slow and golden over the sand like honey. I grabbed my boots and headed that way, following the waterline so I could walk in the wet sand and let the ocean roll over my bare feet, just like he'd said to do.

30

A few hours later, I'd walked the entire beach up and back, explored the area at the bottom of the stairs we'd come down the day before, and found that while there was a restaurant and some little vacation cottages, there was no pay phone anywhere. There were plenty of people around, pretty people who made me wonder if everyone came to eat breakfast on the beach dressed like movie stars. There were also the people who obviously came to enjoy the beach with their families, lugging kids and chairs and coolers along with them. But I hadn't worked up the nerve to ask any of them if I could borrow their cell phone to call my aunt in Texas to bail out my friend who'd been arrested in the parking lot that morning.

Instead, I'd found a wooden picnic table on the sand and claimed it as my own, just in case I was gonna be stuck here for the rest of my life. I stretched out on the bench, eyes closed with my face to the sky, hoping that if I listened hard enough, the universe might take pity on me and whisper something again. It didn't, of course. So after a little while, I stopped listening so hard and just kind of drifted with the sounds of the waves, in and out of the shade from the clouds that passed over the sun, and that way, I was almost able to convince myself that I was here under totally different circumstances. Like maybe a road trip with Lilah or a vacation somewhere tropical or—

"Worried sick, huh?"

I shot up. *"Rusty?"* It was. Standing right over me with one hand in his pocket and a smirk on his face. I didn't think it was humanly possible to be that thankful to see *anyone*, but I was on my feet with my arms wrapped tight around him before he could say another word. There was so much I needed to tell him, I didn't know where to begin. "Oh my god, I'm so, so sorry. For everything. I—and then you—I didn't deserve what you did for me back there," I said, finally getting it out.

Rusty carefully untangled himself from our one-sided hug and stepped a good pace back from me. "Well," he said, digging the toe of his boot in the sand, "you didn't really deserve to hear the things I told you either. Not the way they came out." He looked down, and we were both quiet.

"Don't," I said after a moment. "Don't feel bad about that. What you told me about Finn, it's something I should know. Something that's important for me to know. I just . . ." I took a deep breath and looked at Rusty, surprised at the sudden thickness in my throat. "It's hard for me to understand how he could've done that, you know? How he could've just given up everything he wanted and . . ." I didn't want to cry in front of Rusty again, didn't want him to feel bad for me, so I sat down on the bench and looked out at the ocean. "Why would he do that?"

He sat next to me and let out a big breath as he watched the waves. "I didn't understand when he first told me," he said finally. "I thought he was crazy, thought he was being stupid, and I was pissed at him, and . . . even more pissed at you for it. For a long time." I glanced over at him but didn't say anything. It made perfect sense now, all the times he'd been a jerk or blown me off after Finn enlisted. I probably would've done the same thing to him if I thought Finn had thrown everything away and made the wrong decision because of him.

"It's not so hard to understand though, if you think about how he was," Rusty said. "He loved you. And that's what you do for people you love. You do what you can to help 'em out, give things up if that's what needs to happen. It's not that complicated. Most people just don't go that far, is all." He glanced over at me. "Finn was different from most people."

"Do you think he ever regretted it?" I asked, not wanting him to be honest if the answer was yes.

Rusty shook his head. "No. Once he made his mind up about something, that was it. You know that."

"Kind of like me dragging us all the way out here for Kyra Kelley's show? To tell her about Finn?"

Rusty grinned. "Yeah. Kind of like that."

"We're missing her show, you know. After all that."

"I know," Rusty answered.

A wave broke, filling in the silence that followed. Something in my chest loosened, and I felt a smile rise to my face at the thought of Finn watching our trip play out, all because of his letter. "Can you imagine what he would think of this, though? Of us, in the Pala together?"

Rusty smirked. "He'd be laughing his ass off about you and your straight tequila night, that's for sure."

"Oh god, never bring that up again." I smiled. "Or that kiss."

Rusty cocked his head, and *I* immediately regretted bringing it up. "What kiss?" he asked, like he didn't know. Was he really gonna make me say it?

"At the bar? On the dance floor? I kissed you . . ."

Now it was his turn to laugh. "That . . . never happened."

"Yes it did. I remember, I . . . what do you mean it didn't happen?" Heat rushed up my cheeks. "I *didn't* kiss you?" I didn't know whether to be relieved or disappointed.

Rusty shook his head. "No, you seemed like you might be going for it at one point, but the only thing you kissed that night was the toilet."

"Oh," I said, and it came out sounding definitely more disappointed than relieved. "This whole time I thought—you totally let me think I did." I shook my head, trying to hide just how red my cheeks had gotten. "You're a jerk, you know that?"

"Aw c'mon, H. I just let you think what you wanted to." Rusty turned so that he was facing me. He might've been joking, but in the afternoon light, with the sun in his hair, and the little gold flecks in his eyes, and the ocean in the background, he was right. I wanted to.

"Oh, of *course*," I said, my stomach all fluttery. "Because who wouldn't want to kiss you, right?" It didn't come off nearly as sarcastic as I was going for. *"Please,"* I added. But again, it didn't come through with the right tone.

He just looked at me for a second, the corners of his mouth turned up like he was about to smile. "Since you asked so nice," he said. Then he leaned forward a tiny bit, and I had a moment when I thought, *This is not happening*, but it was. We were. Oh, how we were. His lips just brushed mine at first, but then his hands were in my hair and I was alive all the way to my toes. The whole world could've fallen down around us and I wouldn't have cared, because right then we were the only two in it. It was a kiss that said more than I'd expected—that he knew me, and cared about me, and maybe even . . . I could get carried away by a kiss like that.

Slowly, our lips parted but our faces still hovered almost close enough to touch. I wasn't entirely sure what to do with that moment, and maybe Rusty wasn't either, because he was just looking at me with those green eyes, and I still couldn't believe he'd really kissed me and . . .

"That just happened," I said finally. Out loud.

"Yeah." Rusty cleared his throat and let a smile spread slow and easy across his face. "It sure did."

"Um . . ." I glanced up the beach, suddenly self conscious and with no idea where to go from there. What do you say to someone you just kissed for the first time? Especially when you've known them most of your life and they're your brother's best friend and also a good enough kisser you're pretty sure you may want to do it again? For half a second, I thought Rusty might be thinking the same things and that he might make some joke about it or lean into me again. Something. Maybe. But just as fast as it snuck up on us, the moment was gone.

He leaned forward, resting his elbows on his knees and

putting some space between us. "Listen," he said, suddenly serious. "I had to call Gina to get the registration all straightened out, so I told her where we are and everything." He looked over at me. "You need to talk to her, though."

The fluttery wings in my stomach stopped in midair and spiraled down into a dull feeling of guilt over lying to her. "Is she mad?"

"Worried. But she'll probably be good and mad by the time you talk to her." He nudged me with his shoulder. "You wanna go? Face the music?"

"Not yet." I looked out over the ocean, trying to press the sound and smell and hugeness of it into my memory before I had to turn around and leave it. "Let's go put our feet in the water again first."

Rusty stopped walking and skipped a flat pebble into the sparkling path of sunlight on the ocean. "So you're sure you don't wanna try and see Kyra Kelley? Maybe get backstage? Show's probably not over yet." We both watched as the rock hopped one, two, three times before disappearing into the water.

"I'm sure," I said, and we kept walking. "It'd somehow be a disappointment if I ever got to talk to her anyway. I wouldn't know what to say, or she'd think I was crazy, or maybe she'd be crazy. They are, you know, all those celebrities." I bent to pick up a tiny white shell, then rolled it back and forth between my fingers. "I don't think I really meant to talk to her in the first place, anyway. I am sorry, though, that I didn't get to use those tickets. Who knows what Finn had to do to get them."

A breeze rolled off the water, dragging a few strands of

hair across my face, and I tucked them behind my ear. "But I need to get to Austin. Classes start the day after tomorrow, and I already missed orientation week, and now I don't want to miss any of it. Not when Finn—"

"We can head out tonight if you want," Rusty said.

I stopped walking and turned to him. "I'm gonna take the last of my savings and fly down there." He looked confused, but I'd made up my mind about this. "I want you to take the Pala. You can drive it back to Arizona and have it at school, and it can be yours."

Rusty opened his mouth to interrupt, but I didn't let him. "I thought it all out already. You paid all that money to get it out of the impound lot, and I can pay you back for that eventually, but really, that car belongs with you. You and Finn have more memories in it than I even know about." I paused. "Maybe more than I *wanna* know about." He smiled at this, and I looked down at our bare feet facing each other in the sand. "It'd make him happy knowing you have it. And"—I brought my eyes back up to his—"it'd make me happy too. So you can't say no."

He breathed in deep and looked past me to the ocean, or maybe even past that, all the way back to the days he and Finn spent driving it around Big Lake together, two friends who'd loved and depended on each other and become brothers over the years. Or maybe he was thinking of the hundreds of miles he and I had spent together in the car, through all the things we knew about each other and the things we were surprised to find out, all the while bound together tight by the person Finn had been.

Rusty swallowed hard and looked down at the sand, nodding

like he had just convinced himself. When he brought his eyes back to mine, they were full with the things he didn't say out loud. He didn't need to. It was all laid out there on his face, and I knew it was the right thing to do because I could see how much it meant to him. And because that's what you do when you love someone.

And I did—love Rusty. I loved him in a way that had everything to do with how our past and our present had come together over the miles of highway we'd traveled, how our back then and our now had led us here, to this tiny point on the map. I closed the space between us with a single step and reached my arms around him—a small gesture to tell him so, and he pulled me in close and rested his chin on my head. Standing there together like that felt right as rain, and I knew that after everything, we'd somehow ended up exactly where we were supposed to be. There was no telling where we might find ourselves down the road, but for the moment it didn't matter.

"Thank you," Rusty said into my hair. Then he gently pulled me back by my shoulders and looked past me again.

I turned to see what he was looking at and knew right away. A few feet behind me, lying on its side in the sand like a shipwreck, was one of the lanterns from the ceremony the night before. Rusty and I walked over and he picked it up, inspecting it in the late-afternoon sunlight. Aside from a tear in one side of the paper and a bent corner, it wasn't much worse for the wear. It even had the little candle inside still.

"That's kinda sad it didn't make it with the rest of them," I said, remembering the twinkling lights that had spread out far and wide like stars across the water.

Rusty held it up to the light, inspecting the bottom. "I bet it'd still float." He looked at me then, and I wondered if he knew what I'd been thinking as we watched the ceremony the night before or if he'd been thinking the same thing or knew what I was thinking now. "You wanna send it back out there?" he asked.

A long moment passed before I answered him, and in that time I made up my mind. We could send Finn off from the beach he'd unknowingly guided us to, the two of us. Together. "I think that'd be perfect," I said.

Rusty nodded once in agreement, then kneeled down and set the lantern in the sand. He reached around to his back pocket and pulled out a shiny book of matches with a guitar on the front that I recognized from the bar.

"Wait," I said, reaching for my own back pocket. Rusty looked up, and I slid the letter out, my "real letter" to Finn, with my thank-yous and sorries and stories and hopes scrawled messy on the backs of his pages. And my good-bye. I folded them once more, then kneeled down and slid them between the paper of the lantern and the little wooden frame, tucked in safe and sound for the long trip over the water. "I had a few things to tell him," I said when I looked back to Rusty.

"Hope you told him all the good parts," he said with a smile. Then he pulled a match out and lit it, holding the small flame between us. "You wanna say anything?"

I hadn't noticed any tears creeping up on me, but they were there now. I breathed in deep and shook my head. Rusty touched the match to the candle's wick, setting the whole lantern aglow with soft, white light. Then he waved the match out and nodded at me to do the honors. I took one more deep breath, then lifted the lantern in my hands and stood up. We walked the few paces down to the water's edge, then stood still and quiet a moment, nothing but the lantern and the gentle whoosh of the waves between us.

This was it. This was the moment to say good-bye and send Finn off. From the beach, with my toes in the water, standing next to the only other person in the world who knew and loved him as much as I did. I stepped a few paces farther into the cool water, sinking into the soft sand below it, and when I was far enough I thought he could make it past the ripples, I lowered the lantern to the ocean and gave it a gentle push.

Rusty stepped up beside me then and put his arm around my shoulders, and I leaned into him without thinking about it. Neither one of us said anything. We just stood there together with our feet in the ocean, watching the lantern drift slowly toward the setting sun, its tiny flickering light barely visible. And we stayed there like that until we couldn't see it anymore, but I knew it was on its way across the ocean to the horizon, where the sun dripped gold into the water and peace lit the sky up pink.

Rusty can't come with me any farther. We stand off to the side of the security screening area as passengers whisk by with their wheeled suitcases and file into line to be inspected. He doesn't pay any attention to them—just stands there looking at me in a way that makes me wanna forget my plane ticket and get back in the Pala with him. But I know that's not supposed to be, so instead I stand on my tiptoes and wrap my arms around his neck and tuck my head close.

"I'm gonna miss you," I say. And I think I might cry, so I

bury my face farther into the space between his neck and his shoulder.

He brings a hand to my neck, gives it a squeeze beneath my hair. "Yeah." He sighs. "You really are."

It's enough to make me laugh, and I push away from him, no longer at the edge of tearing up. "Well I'm glad you're gonna be all right."

He smiles and looks down at the shiny floor before bringing his eyes back up to mine. "I'm gonna miss you too, H. I am." A woman's voice calls out flight numbers above us and says something I can't make out above the bustle of the airport. Rusty clears his throat and shoves his hands in his pockets. "You better get going," he says. "Just in case she's talking about yours."

"Yeah. I should . . ." *Kiss you one last time? Tell you to come with me? Drive home with you?* "I should go," I say, and I hitch my purse up on my shoulder like I'm gonna walk away, but I stay right where I am. "So . . . drive careful and . . ." I give him another quick hug, then a kiss on his scruffy cheek. "And I love you." There's a second of quiet, and I can tell he doesn't know what to say, so I don't wait for him to answer. I turn on my heel and head toward the end of the security line, feeling him watch me as I go, and hoping he knows I meant it. When I finally do turn around, it's just in time to see his silhouette making its way through the crowd, back out to the road and school and football, where he's supposed to be. And maybe . . . maybe one day back to me.

The line in front of me is crowded with people holding their tickets and IDs in one hand and taking off their shoes and belts with the other. Suddenly nervous, I take a cue and open my purse to dig out my wallet. The line inches forward faster than I thought it would, and of course now I can't seem to slide my license out from behind the plastic cover. I wiggle it and pull at the same time, and it finally slides free, along with everything else, all over the floor.

"Oh geez, I'm sorry," I say to the guy behind me. "Go ahead." I stoop to pick up the contents of my wallet, and two more people step over me like I'm not even there.

"Here, I think this is yours." A manicured hand reaches down to me, holding a picture I didn't even remember I had.

"Thank you," I say, taking it without looking up. I smile at the image in my hands: me, Finn, and Rusty all leaning on the Pala, against a backdrop of bright blue Texas sky. Gina took it the day the boys brought it home, all proud and full of themselves and their plans for the car, and I'd talked my way into the picture, sure I belonged next to it just as much as they did.

"They're cute," the same voice from behind me says. "They your friends? Boyfriends?"

I stand up, trying to tuck everything back in my purse. "No," I say as I turn. "The one in the cowboy hat's my brother, and the other one's . . ."

The girl who belongs to the voice smiles from beneath the brim of her baseball cap, waiting for me to finish, but I don't. I can't. I've completely forgotten what I was going to say because I'd know that smile and those sparkly blue eyes anywhere.

"Your brother, huh?" Kyra Kelley raises a perfectly arched eyebrow. "I've always had a thing for cowboys." She smiles. "That whole gentlemanly thing, you know?"

I nod but don't say anything. Kyra Kelley is standing behind me in line at the airport. Talking to me.

"Big difference from the LA boys, that's for sure. I'm finished with them, if you know what I mean." She pauses and looks at me—really looks at me, then winks. "But your cute cowboy brother . . . he looks like he might be one you should tell me about. If you've got the time, of course."

And I do. Oh, how I do.

Acknowledgments

I find myself once again marveling at the fact that I am fortunate enough to know and work with such amazing people—and feeling like I don't have the right words to convey just how much gratitude I have for that. Nevertheless, I will try!

First off, I would like to thank my agent, Leigh Feldman, for her encouragement, guidance, honesty, and the magic ability to give each exactly when I need it most. I am so, so lucky to have her and her lovely assistant, Jean Garnett, by my side each step of the way. I am just as lucky to have the wisdom and dedication of Alexandra Cooper, my editorial match made in heaven. Her ability to see right through to the heart of the story, and then cast a light on the many routes to get there is truly amazing and something I am incredibly grateful for.

I owe a huge thank-you to Justin Chanda and the entire Simon & Schuster team, including Ariel Coletti, Paul Crichton, Laura Antonacci, Michelle Fadlalla, Lydia Finn, Amy Rosenbaum, and Venessa Williams for their support, enthusiasm, and dedication. It means so much to be able to work with people who are so passionate about what they do.

To Krista Vossen and the art department at S&S, thank you, thank you, thank you for granting my cover wish and then making it more perfect than I could have possibly imagined!

To my family and friends, your endless support and love mean more than the world to me, and all the best moments in my life are because of you.

Above all, my deepest gratitude belongs to Schuyler—my best friend, my husband, my heart. Thank you for your belief in and patience with me, for your perfect ideas and smart, true advice, and for all of the very real conversations about my very imaginary characters. There would be no Honor or Rusty without you.

Reading Group Guide

1. Honor takes a spur-of-the-moment road trip to cope with the pain of losing her brother, Finn. What do you normally do to deal with being sad? If you have lost someone close to you, how did you try to cope with that loss?
2. Have you ever done something impulsive like Honor does? What were the consequences of your action? If you had the choice to make again, would you do the same thing?
3. Finn and Honor have a superclose sibling relationship because of their shared past. Do you have any sisters or brothers? Do you get along? What is one of your favorite shared memories?
4. Have you known anyone who enlisted in the military? How did you react to his or her decision?
5. Rusty and Finn were best friends, but Rusty stops talking to Finn after he joins the marines. Have you ever stopped speaking to a friend? How do you feel about your decision now?
6. If you could take a road trip anywhere in the United States, where would you go? Why? Who would you take?
7. Kyra Kelley is Honor's favorite singer in the entire world. If you could see any concert by any band or singer, current or past, who would you see? Why?
8. Honor initially dislikes Rusty based on his cocky attitude and her belief that he abandoned Finn, but she gives him a second chance when the facts later come to light.

Have you ever made a snap judgment about someone and then realized you might have been wrong? What did you base your first impression on, and what caused you to revise it later?

9. Honor is reluctant to scuba dive at Blue Hole in New Mexico, but she changes her mind when she realizes that it's "exactly the type of thing Finn would have done" and would have convinced her to do too. Who in your life encourages you to take risks on new experiences? What have you done that you might not have attempted without someone else's encouragement? How did you feel after this experience?
10. When Honor meets Ashley and her mother on the vortex tour, she learns that Kyra Kelley is Ashley's cousin. Have you ever had a moment of serendipity like this? What was the result?
11. Honor's red cowboy boots are her signature look. Do you have an article of clothing that means a lot to you? How did you get it?

Parker Frost is about to take the road less traveled by.

Turn the page for a sneak peek at Jessi Kirby's third novel!

life is made of moments. and choices.

Not all of them matter, or have any lasting impact. Skipping class in favor of a taste of freedom, picking a prom dress because of the way it transforms you into a princess in the mirror. Even the nights you steal away from an open window, tiptoe silent to the end of the driveway, where darkened headlights and the pull of something unknown beckon. These are all small choices, really. Insignificant as soon as they're made. Innocent.

But then.

Then there's a different kind of moment. One when things are irrevocably changed by a choice we make. A moment we will play endlessly in our minds on lonely nights and empty days. One we'll search repeatedly for some indication that what we chose was right, some small sign that tells us the truth isn't nearly as awful as it feels. Or as awful as anyone would think if they knew.

So we explain it to ourselves, justify it enough to sleep. And then we bury it deep, so deep we can almost pretend it never happened. But as much as we wish it were different, the truth is, our worlds are sometimes balanced on choices we make and the secrets we keep.

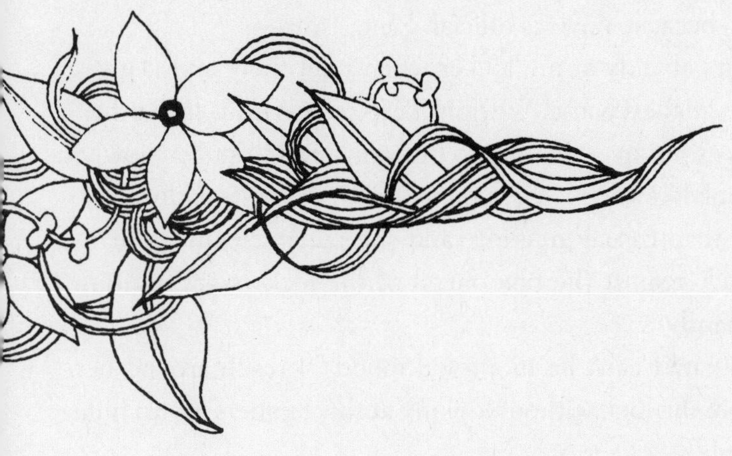

"To a Thinker"

—1936

There's no such thing as a secret in this town. But I'm keeping this one, just for today. I fold the letter once, twice, three times and slide it into my back pocket like a golden ticket, because that's what it is. A ticket out. Being chosen as a finalist for the Cruz-Farnetti Scholarship is my version of winning the lottery. It means Stanford pre-med and everything else I've worked for.

Icy wind sears my cheeks red as I cross the school parking lot, and I curse Johnny Mountain for being right when he forecast the late spring storm. If the biting wind and swirling white sky are any indication, we may be graduating in the snow, which is not at all how I pictured it. But today I don't *really* mind. Today the wind and I burst through the double doors together, and it carries me like someone who's going places, because now it's official. I am.

Kat's already at my locker when I get there and it gives me the smallest pause. We don't keep secrets from each other. Her eyes run over me, top to bottom, and she smiles slowly. "*You* look like you're in a good mood." It's more friendly accusation than casual greeting, and she punctuates it by leaning back against the blue metal of the lockers and waiting expectantly.

"What? I can't be in a good mood?" I reach around her and spin the lock without looking at the numbers, try to hide my smile.

She shrugs and steps aside. "*I'm* not. This weather sucks. Mountain says it's gonna be the worst storm in ten years or some bullshit like that. I'm *so* over the frickin' snow. It's May. We should be wearing tiny shorts and tank tops instead of . . . this." She looks down at her outfit in disdain.

"Well," I say, trying to pull my mind away from visions of the red-tiled roofs and snowless breezeways of Stanford, "you look cute anyway."

Kat rolls her eyes, but straightens up her shoulders the slightest bit and I know that's exactly what she wanted to hear. She stands there looking effortless in her skinny jeans, tall boots, and a top that falls perfectly off one shoulder, revealing a lacy black bra strap. Really, cute isn't the right word for her. The last time she was cute was probably elementary school. By the time we hit seventh grade, she was hot and all its variations, for a couple more reasons than just her tumbling auburn hair. That was the year Trevor Collins nicknamed the two of us "fire and ice," and it stuck. In the beginning I thought the whole "ice" thing had something to do with my last name (Frost), or maybe my eyes (blue), but over the years, it's become increasingly clear that's not what he meant. At all.

Kat shuts my locker with a flick of her wrist as soon as I unlock it. "So. There's a sub for Peters today, a cute one I'd normally stick around for, but I'm starving and Lane's working at Kismet. Let's get outta here and eat. He'll give us free drinks and I'll have you back by second period. Promise." She's about to come up with another inarguable reason for me to ditch with her when Trevor Collins strolls up. Even after this long, that's still how I think of him. Trevor Collins. It was how he introduced himself when he walked into Lakes High in seventh grade with a winning smile, natural charm, and the confidence to match.

His eyes flick to me, not Kat, and heat blooms in my cheeks. "Hey, Frost. You look saucy today. Feelin' adventurous?" He dangles a lanyard in front of me, and a smile hovers at the corners of his mouth. "I got the keys to the art supply closet, and *I* could have you back before first period even starts. Promise." He hits me with a smile that lets me know he's joking, but I wonder for a second what would happen if I actually said yes one of these days.

I meet his eyes, barely, before opening my locker so the door creates a little wall between us, then give my best imitation of disinterested sarcasm. "Tempting." But between his dyed black hair and crystal blue eyes, it kind of is. I have no doubt a trip to the art supply closet with him would be an experience. Half the female population at Lakes High would probably attest to it, which is exactly why it'll never happen. I like to think of it as principle. And standards. Besides, this has been our routine since we were freshmen, and I like it this way, with possibility still dancing between us. From what I've seen, it's almost always better than reality.

Kat blows him a kiss meant to send him on his way. "She can't. We're going to get coffee. And she's too good for you. And you have a girlfriend, jackass." There's that, too, I remind myself. But I've never really counted Trevor's girlfriends as legitimate, seeing as they don't generally last beyond being given the title.

"Actually, I'm not," I say a little too abruptly. "Going to get coffee, I mean." I shut my locker and Trevor raises an eyebrow, jingling his keys. "I uh . . . I can't skip Kinney's today. He's got some big project for me." Oh, the lameness.

Kat rolls her eyes emphatically. "You don't *actually* have to show up to class when you're the TA and it's last quarter. You do realize that, right?"

"*You* don't have to," I say, matching her smart-ass tone, "because Chang has no idea she even has a TA. Kinney actually realizes I'm supposed to be there."

The bell rings and Trevor takes a step backward, holding up the keys again. "Best four minutes you ever had, Frost. Going once, twice . . ."

I wave him off with a grin, then turn back to Kat, who's now giving me her *you know you want to* look. "Never," I say. I know what's coming next, and I'm hoping that's enough to squash it.

But it's not, because as we walk, she bumps my hip with hers. "C'mon, P. You know you want to. *He's* wanted to since forever."

"Only because *I* haven't."

"Maybe," she shrugs. "But still. School's gonna end, you're gonna wish that just once, you'd done something I would do."

I stop at Mr. Kinney's doorway. Now it's me with the smile. "You mean *did*, right? Because I distinctly remember my best friend being the first girl here to kiss Trevor Collins."

"That was in seventh grade. That doesn't even count." A slow smile spreads over her lips. "Although for a seventh grader, he was a pretty good kisser."

I just look at her.

"Fine," Kat says in her dramatic Kat way that communicates her ongoing disappointment every time I plant my feet firmly on the straight and narrow road. "Go to class. Spend the last few weeks of your senior year pining over the guy you could have in a second while you're at it. I'll see you later." She smacks me on the butt as she leaves, right where my letter is, and for a second I feel guilty about not telling her because this letter means that Stanford has gone from far-off possibility to probable reality. But leaving Kat is also a reality at this point, and I don't think either one of us is ready to think about that yet.

When I step through Kinney's door, future all folded up in my back pocket, he's headed straight for me with an ancient-looking box. "Parker! Good. I'm glad you're here. Take these." He practically throws the box into my arms.

"Senior class journals, like I told you about. It's time to send them out." His eyes twinkle the tiniest bit when he says it, and that's the reason kids love him. He keeps his promises.

I nod, because that's all I have time to do before he goes on. Kinney drinks a lot of coffee. "I want you to go through them like we talked about. Double-check the addresses against the directory, which'll probably take you all week, then get whatever extra postage they need so I can send them out by the end of the month, okay?" He's a little out of breath by the time he finishes, but that's how he always is, because he's high-strung in the best kind of way. The million miles a minute, jump up on the table in the middle of teaching to make a point kind of way.

Before I can ask any questions, he's stepped past me to hold the door open for the sleepy freshmen filing in. Most of them look less than excited for first period, but Mr. Kinney stands there with his wide smile, looks each one of them in the eye, and says "Good morning," and even the grouchy-looking boys with their hoods pulled up say it back.

"Mr. Kinney?" I lug the box of journals a few steps so I'm out of their way. "Would you mind if I take these to the library to work on them?"

"Not at all." He winks and ushers me on my way with the swoop of an arm. "See you at the end of the period." Right on cue, the final bell rings and he swings his classroom door shut without another word.

I linger a moment in the emptied hallway and peek through the skinny window in his door as students get out their notebooks to answer the daily writing prompt they've become accustomed to by this point in the year. Sometimes it's a question, sometimes a quote or artwork he throws out there for them to explain. Today it's a poem, one I'm deeply familiar with, since my dad has always claimed we're somehow, *possibly*, long-lost, distant relatives of the poet himself.

I read the eight lines slowly, even though I know them by heart. Today though, they hang differently in my mind—too heavily. Maybe it's the unwelcome, swirling wind outside, or the fact that so much in my life is about to change, but as I read them, I feel like I have to remind myself that just because someone wrote them doesn't make them true. I would never want to believe they were true. Because according to Robert Frost, "nothing gold can stay."